# A Life Quite Ordinary

Campbell Johnston

First published in 2025 by Blossom Spring Publishing
A Life Quite Ordinary Copyright © 2025 Campbell Johnston
ISBN 978-1-917938-15-0
E: admin@blossomspringpublishing.com
W: www.blossomspringpublishing.com
All rights reserved under International Copyright Law.
Contents and/or cover may not be reproduced in whole
or in part without the express written consent
of the publisher.
Names, characters, places and incidents
are either products of the author's imagination
or are used fictitiously.

For the future, which is in such safe hands:

Emily, Ben, Howard, Zoe, Elina, Amara, Rory, Olivia, Adele, Sam, Paloma, Rafferty, Charlotte, Ed, Oscar

To: Gina Stein-Noble GST@crepuscularfilms.com
Cc: heidi123@gsmile.co.uk

Hi Gina,

Thank you so much for your email. As discussed, I attach the bundle of papers that my father, Gordon, kept in a box in our attic (knotted in his old school tie). The papers record the story of my Dad's early life and his relationship with of your uncle, Lord Haston-Cross of Cuddamore. My father took much of the story from his diary and the notes from your uncle. He persuaded my mother, Caroline, to add her recollections. Peter Hardy had his arm twisted by his wife, Sheena and your late Papa, Sir A P Stein, added the rest. I am not sure why, but they almost seem to be drafted as witness statements.

I have kept everything in the same order that my father had them before he died but I have separated them into "attachments" to make them easier to send and read. I have included your Papa's notes on the "top secret" document (attachment 15). It was clever of you to have found Brigadier Pardue through his regimental association so he could fill in the gap. I have put my father's introductions in italics so you can delete them if necessary. Father did so want to write a book from the bundle, but there was always something to sort at the Old Rectory and he never found time.

It is still hard to believe that my father was involved in such delicate matters; matters that touched on the defence of the realm. I am incredulous that he was accused of treason!

I am delighted that you have been able to secure from Peter Hardy the extra funding for the film of your uncle's remarkable life. Peter is a very generous man, but it does not surprise me that he wants no publicity.

I am thrilled that Quentin has agreed to be a co-producer. Heidi (my sister) and I should love to meet him when, as you have suggested, there is an "opening night".

If I can assist any further, please do not hesitate to contact me.

Kind regards
*Raich Shawcross*

Attachments

| | |
|---|---|
| Gordon Shawcross | 1,5,10,12,16,25,27,29,31 |
| Peter (Geordie) Hardy | 2,7,11 |
| Caroline Jervis | 3,14 |
| Ryan Haston (Sean Cross) | 4,6,9,20,22,26,28,30 |
| Anthony P Stein | 8,13,17,18,21,23,24. |
| Note from the Brigadier | 15 |
| Quentin McCrae | 19 |

## Attachment 1

## Mnemonics

**Gordon Shawcross**

Ryan Haston was the school bully, but he avoided me. He surrounded himself with fawning acolytes, all ready to do his bidding, but he was careful that they did not cross my path. Whilst this may give the impression that I am some heavyweight, nothing could be further from the truth. I can hardly carry my own shoulder blades. He did bully me, along with everyone else, for the first few terms, but there was an incident when I was about fifteen when I took prompt action that probably saved Ryan Haston's life. It meant that after that, I had a very peaceful, stress-free, incident-free school existence. Ryan Haston was tall, blond, athletic, and clever and I was never sure why he was a bully at the time. I know now, but then that is the great thing about hindsight and of course it helped that Ryan told me. Even after all these years, he needs to keep in contact.

Every Roman schoolboy knew the mnemonic "SALIGIA"; it was the initials of the seven deadly sins: Superbia, Avaritia, Luxuria, Invidia, Gula, Ira, Acedia. For those without Latin: pride, greed, lust, envy, gluttony, anger, and sloth. To have had any of these cardinal sins would have been considered a defect in character and, in all likelihood, led that Roman schoolboy to have a miserable life. I was not a Roman schoolboy. I enjoyed my Classics but could not keep anything in my head. Mnemonics helped me remember the mnemonic but knowing the letters was not enough, you needed to know what the letters meant. I would never learn the seven deadly sins, but little did I know that over the next few decades I would be visited by most of them.

Every Friday, last lesson, without fail, school would draw to a close with "the sevens". Starting with seven Classics questions, then seven spelling questions, seven general knowledge questions and seven mathematics questions and various other sevens; well, you get the gist. Seventy questions at four o'clock every Friday. If you managed to get forty-nine (70 per cent) correct, you could leave the school immediately for the weekend. Less than forty-nine and you stayed for an extra twenty-one questions which took at least an extra half hour. I lived my life at base seven. I had to pass the first part, as failure meant missing the number 255 bus home. I would then have to wait an hour for the number 250X. This was the express which neatly by-passed my village by three miles and meant a miserable run home from the nearest bus stop.

Whilst I could never remember the deadly sins, I did remember the seven virtues. There is no doubt that my all-boys grammar school placed less emphasis on the virtues, probably because they were less interesting. For me, if the Friday quiz seven Classics questions started with "name the seven virtues", I was confident I would be on the early bus home. As this is not a pub quiz, the virtues were: charity, loyalty, humility, honesty, diligence, patience and kindness. I did not even need a mnemonic for this, but I am sure that in trying to figure out the best way of remembering these qualities, they stayed in my brain, if not as subsequent events showed, in my actions.

We were at a school that considered cricket and rugby to be integral to the education. We had two "rival" grammar schools within 25 miles. One had only been created in the 1930s, so was not a major threat, but the other was founded in 1591, a mere 30 years after our school, so there was always some serious history at stake, especially on the playing fields. Whilst I would not wish to suggest we had discipline like Tom Brown experienced at his school, there was corporal punishment. It was never used to punish you for doing something naughty. Being naughty just resulted in more academic work. Punishment was reserved for character defects. We once lost a cricket match, having only scored 11 runs as a team. The fact that the victorious "1591" school had a bowler that would one day captain Yorkshire was of no matter. We had not shown enough grit. I was always perplexed as to why "grit" was not on the list of virtues, but then the Romans were from Rome, not Yorkshire. Geoff Farnthwait, the

Deputy Head, responsible for discipline, had the whole cricket team up to his office where we were admonished in a hectoring rant. He never looked at us. His gaze never left the window. He never saw us as individuals, just a spineless group. We all received six of the best. I had scored four as the prize bowler had hit my bat whilst I frantically tried to defend my body and the ball had shot past the wicketkeeper to the boundary. As the highest scorer, I felt some pride and defiance whilst suffering my fate. I was also still laughing at Robert Nixon's situation. He got six strikes of the cane and he had been the twelfth man. He had not even picked up a bat. He had only been the scorer during the match. I have often wondered whether Robert's luck had improved in life. I did hear he became an accountant so perhaps that was the ultimate punishment for him.

I have mentioned how weedy I was, but I could run fast, probably more from the enforced three-mile Friday runs from the bus stop than anything else. I was always stuck out on the wing for the rugby season and was just swift and able enough to avoid the most violent opposition forwards. At the end of the season, we played sevens (naturally) and this culminated in a three-way tournament with our rival schools. As it was towards the end of term, there was a carnival atmosphere. It was usually warm weather and as each match was only 20 minutes, it built up to be quite an exciting day. The parents, staff, and pupils from all the schools would come to watch.

I found myself in the second seven, more through the high dropout rate of the good players through injury at that stage of the season, than any particular skill. We did have Ryan Haston and Robert Nixon and a new boy who was a Geordie called Hardy. Geordie (I never knew his first name when we were at school) had only ever played football before joining the school. Haston did not like him and he did not like Haston.

Inexplicably, I had been made captain by Chub Richards, our rugby teacher. He said that I was the least likely and therefore the most likely. When I asked what this meant, his only reply was 'exactly'! One of our team strengths was that Haston would never pass to Geordie and vice versa. It always confused the opposition when the absolute obvious (even scoring) pass was eschewed by either of them for some other hapless member of our team who was usually surprised to receive the pass.

I will not go into too many details about the tournament, save that we got to the semi-final where we were due to meet our "A" team. Our "A" team was called Rievaulx. We were Jervaulx, named after two famous Yorkshire abbeys. Geoff Farnthwait, the Deputy Head, came over to me before the start of the match and asked how I thought we would fare against our stronger "A" team. He did not ask for an answer, but mused that the school must put up the best team in the final to beat 1591. He stressed that there could be glory in defeat. He mentioned the gallant 300 at Thermopylae. He quoted Tennyson and the charge of the Light Brigade. He started to talk about Trafalgar and then corrected himself and muttered about Nelson. I found myself walking alongside him as we wandered towards the edge of the school quadrant. He stopped and turned me towards him with his hands on both my shoulders.

'Well, what do you think of defeat, Shawcross?' he said. I pondered, his heavy hands were bearing down and I could smell tobacco on his breath. I suddenly realised what he was asking of me. He wanted me to throw the match.

I pulled my shoulders back and said, 'Yes sir, I remember what you said after the cricket match, you do not mind defeat as long as we show "grit". I can assure you, Jervaulx will either win or go down fighting.' He removed his hands. He held my stare.

He said menacingly, 'If you do win this one, you had jolly well better win the final.' He turned to walk away; his Parthian shot was to tell me to get my feet off the grass; I was standing on the precious quadrant.

I remembered Hippocrates and wondered if he had anything to do with hypocrite. We did not win the semi-final, mainly because of the fight which resulted in two members of Jervaulx being sent off. Yes, somewhat predictably, Geordie and Haston; both blamed each other for a ball that dropped between them that neither picked up. It took all the remaining players and several spectators, including Farnthwait, to separate them. Rievaulx went on to lose the final and fittingly blamed their tough semi-final and the disruptive fight for their loss of form. Farnthwait was apoplectic.

It was the sevens tournament that did alter my life somewhat. The captain of the 1591 team could have been my doppelganger. When we stood together, we were completely different but strangely when we were apart, people would often confuse us. Everyone asked if we were related. Even the chap's form-master who shouted 'Jervis' to me and then apologised when I turned towards him. Mark Jervis was from Corton Grammar and lived some 25 miles away. His father was a consultant at the cottage hospital. We chatted as we watched the final and I did enjoy his company. He suggested that I bring over my "team" to his house for a party on the next Saturday evening. I said it was too far, but he prevailed upon my sense of adventure and I relented. I would go if my team would agree to come with me. He assured me that his father allowed drink, and we could camp in his garden. Haston and Geordie were both feeling rather proud of themselves after the semi-final fight spectacle and were keen to go. So it was that seven teenage boys with absolutely nothing in common, save for Jervaulx Abbey, planned to go to Corton.

We had decided to leave Saturday morning, but Morton had a paper-round and Nixon had to milk cows on his father's farm. Haston assumed leadership and told everyone that the rest of us would go without them. Geordie said he was waiting for them and 'in any case Shawcross was in charge as he was the captain.' I was somewhat flattered by this appointment but reminded myself *no pride*.

I told them it was 'All for one and one for all,' or something along those lines. In the event, Turner could not go because it was too far and Hetherington simply did not show. So, we five did set off mid-afternoon, bus to Middlesbrough, train to Darlington and bus to Corton. This sounds straightforward but it was actually a three-hour mission with much hanging around and much grumbling. We did ask about buses back to Darlington when we finally alighted the last bus to Corton at six thirty. We were told it would be a Sunday service which sounded reasonable. We should have known that if the last bus on a Saturday was six thirty, then Sunday would mean no buses.

We arrived at the Old Vicarage and whilst Mark was pleased to see us, his parents, who were just leaving, seemed less so. Dr Jervis climbed out of his car and nodded to us coldly and then specifically reminded Mark that they were only in the next village and would be home by 10 o'clock. As parties go, it was better than most we were used to. The house was huge, and the food was spread over a long, wide farmhouse table. Drink was plentiful and everyone seemed in good spirits. I suggested erecting the tent so it would be ready when we needed it, but was persuaded that this was far too early and that everyone would help when the time came. Nixon and Morton grabbed two table-tennis bats that were propped on a ball on a table-tennis table and started playing. Haston fell in with some 1591 school "rugger buggers" who recognised him from the fight and so he left our group. This delighted Geordie who had become increasingly socialist, moaning about Mark's middle-class privileges, the splendour of the house and the waste of food. The house was crowded and I was pleased to throw off Geordie when he saw the record collection piled up behind the disco and he went off to help the DJ.

I was rather happy to be on my own. I picked up a can of lager from the drinks table, a sausage roll from the food table and strolled into the conservatory. It was huge, like everything else in the house, and had exotic palms and wicker type chairs. I also thought how Geordie had such a different view on life to me. He was angry that they had a fancy house and begrudged them it, whereas I wanted a house like this one day.

I suppose it was just our view of the future and our politics were being shaped. Geordie hated the fact we were at a grammar school and we were part of the elite. It had not even crossed my mind how lucky or privileged we were. I flopped down on a Lloyd Loom chair, similar but larger to one that my Nan had in her kitchen.

I was startled when a girl appeared between two rubber plants and said, 'Very interesting... but stupid! Oh! Mark, why are you all alone?'

I stood up and she said, 'Oh sorry, I thought you were Mark. Well, how weird,' she smiled, 'not recognising my own brother!'

'Have you been drinking?' I joked, but felt self-conscious. I explained who I was and said that Mark's form-master had made the same mistake, so Mark and I were clearly similar. We both agreed that whilst there was no specific feature that was the same, altogether we were strangely alike. Whether it was the similarity to her brother or the fact that I was a stranger, we started chatting and continued to do so for what seemed an hour. We were interrupted several times by Caroline's friends checking she was fine. Most seemed quite content with a short introduction before departing. I tried to be gallant and suggested that she might want to go and meet someone more interesting but thankfully, she declined and said she liked talking to me because I was interesting and not stupid.

I was starting to worry that the conversation would dry up and I would be exposed as a bumbling fool, when there was a huge commotion from the main room. Girls were screaming and there were shouts of anguish. Caroline and I ran through to find Haston prostrate and having convulsions on the floor. Someone had their hand on his mouth. Someone was shouting 'Squeeze his back! squeeze his back!'

I thought, *Oh God, Haston is choking. He has swallowed something.* His eyes were bulging and he was going blue. He was shaking as if he was having a fit. His mouth was bright orange.

A girl next to me said, 'He tried to put the full orange in his mouth and it got stuck behind his teeth.'

I did not stop to think. I grabbed a cheese knife off the table and rushed to Haston. I pulled away a boy who was trying to prize open Haston's jaws wider and plunged the knife into the orange trapped in Haston's mouth. I gouged out the soft fruit middle. Haston was being sick and the orange was being forced out with brown vomit. I continued to wrestle the crushed orange out of his mouth. I tried to sit him up and was assisted by several pairs of hands. Haston spluttered and groaned. He bit my knuckle and I thought at least he can close his jaw. Someone offered him water, but he was too confused, so I used the water to wash his face. He started crying; not just sobs but almost wailing. He was hugging me. The room was silent. Geordie, who was manning the record decks, had sensibly taken off the record. I saw him give me a thumbs up. Caroline was at my shoulder and behind them, looming large, was Dr Jervis.

The doctor pointed at me and asked, 'What drugs has he taken? I need to know.' I looked at Haston. There was no evidence of the orange which had fallen to his side, nor the actual cause of the problem.

'He does not take drugs,' I lamely offered.

'I shall be the judge,' said Dr Jervis, who was now feeling Haston's pulse and looking into his eyes and eyelids. 'Clear the party, Caroline,' ordered the Doctor. No-one needed much encouragement and everyone started to drift off. An ambulance arrived for Haston. Whilst it was not needed, given that Haston may have fitted, he was dispatched off anyway. I did try and explain to Mrs Jervis what had happened, but I was "with Haston" and so was more guilty than he was as I had not stopped him. Geordie told Mrs Jervis that I had saved Haston's life, but he told her in such an aggressive manner that we both got a further lecture on behaviour as a guest in someone else's house.

So, we four found ourselves in a quiet Yorkshire

village in the middle of the night with nowhere to stay. We all agreed that the village green was too exposed, and we would get into trouble staying there. We were quite upbeat when we found a green field next to the church that seemed flat, but any elation was crushed when we realised Haston had the tent poles. It was a long cold night, four of us sleeping on and under canvas. Geordie had some concerns that we might be in the graveyard and that caused some stress. I had to get out from under the canvas, as I was on the end, to confirm that we were the only bodies in the field. We did re-christen Haston "Jaffa" and that made us laugh. Things did not get any better the next day. There was no bus to Darlington, and it took us most of the day to walk there. The train to Middlesbrough was a replacement bus service. When I eventually got home, late Sunday, it was to face my mother's wrath. I would always prefer to be scolded by my father as it was always short and sharp, whereas Mother could drag an issue out for months.

# Attachment 2

# Snobs

*New undergraduates at Oxford and Cambridge in the 16th Century had to register both their name and rank on enrolment. If they were neither titled nor held a rank, they put* sine nobilitate *(without nobility). This was usually abbreviated to "snob". Nowadays in our "egalitarian society" most people are somewhat reluctant to state their class. Despite this, an accent, a tattoo or a Rolex Oyster is often enough to indicate social status. We are genetically programmed to want more for our children than we have had ourselves and perhaps this is the crampon that assists us in our social climbing. That said, it never quite explains social abseilers, nor Americans, who never quite get our obsession with class.*

*One American who did understand was Eleanor Roosevelt; her observation perhaps identified the real differences between classes. 'Great minds discuss ideas. Average minds discuss events. Small minds discuss people'. Traditionally the upper classes had the leisure time that allowed them to explore philosophy and creative thought – they seemingly had the great minds. The middle class had to earn money, so they tended to lead the armed forces, the church and the professions. The middle class had time to plan the events, and were often paid to take part, whether it was wars, elections, or festivals. The working class could only discuss people. The working class were given the least scope for developing their minds with the poorest of education and the least chance to move from their station.*

*Following that logic, perhaps society should now have changed. It has been the unemployed that have had the most leisure time and there has been almost universal access to education, so why has this not produced the great minds of the last two decades? Background and breeding have been no bar to unlimited wealth, particularly if you can kick a football or sell Amstrad computers. But perhaps we have not moved on. The new upper class, the bankers, discuss imaginative "swaps and derivatives". These are seemingly just paper ideas, as they have been shown to have no actual value. The new middle class discuss events, hence the disappointment in not winning the Eurovision Song Contest and the disinterested argue about soap operas.*

## Peter (Geordie) Hardy

Numbers were second nature to me. I could count before I could say a sentence. My party trick, before I could walk, was to add up in twos and threes and count backwards. The only person who showed any interest in me was Mandy, my social worker. Mandy was probably the only person who realised that I was gifted. My grandmother tried to give me some attention, but she had her hands full with my mother and her four younger siblings. Although I did not know it then, had I subtracted my age from that of my mother, the answer would have been 13.

One aunt was only four years older than I was and there were no men in the house and never seemed to have been. I was a lonely child and learnt early that keeping quiet was always the answer. I did enjoy singing but all the early tunes were from my grandma's memory. I knew Cushie Butterfield.

*She was a braw lass and a bonnie lass*
*and she liked her beer*
*and they called her Cushie Butterfield*
*and I do wish she was here*

I could chant the tale of young Geordie Lampton who *caught the worm with big googly eyes when he went fishin… down upon the Wear.*

My mother was never going to cope with me. She was just a child herself, so I was farmed out initially to helpful neighbours. I was "no bother, like", and this worked for a while but it was never going to be right for the "social", who took me into care. It was Mandy who recommended that I be fostered by a kindly family in Whitley Bay that she knew. I did not know then, but I was just young enough to learn to speak in an accent that could be understood by most northern folk. Before this, my only talk had been with my close family so I picked up their poor diction and pronunciation and then added a couple of layers of my own.

Ray and Jean, my foster parents, were snobs. They had no children of their own and I think I helped confirm their position that children were a necessary evil and that they had dodged the bullet by not being able to have any of their own. Ray introduced me to football and as the first man in my life, I was grateful to hear his thoughts on football and many other topics. He was happy to chat to me about anything when the two of us were together, but he had nothing at all to say in the presence of Jean. They seemed to be happy, but they did not seem to talk to each other. I gleaned from Ray that they fostered me because Jean played bowls with Mandy who had promised that I was a remarkable child. Jean wanted to be seen to help the less fortunate and underprivileged and thought I could be a project. I am not sure Ray had any say in their decision. I was Jean's act of charity. Perhaps I should have been angered by this revelation, but I was just grateful for the clean house and regular meals. Jean had been a hospital financial administrator but became a housewife to look after me. Jean was numerate and so the one thing that we could seriously bond over was mathematics. I awakened a latent passion in her and we could spend hours doing maths puzzles and questions; an activity that must have seemed bizarre to anyone used to conventional parenting. Ray worked for the railways, so the other novelty that I was introduced to was travel and railway timetables. Ray had a free pass and so at every opportunity we went off on train journeys, usually for a day, but occasionally when the railways had a special deal, we stayed over in Leeds or on one memorable trip, Edinburgh. For one birthday they gave me a Timex watch. Ray said that I would never have an excuse for missing a train. I was thrilled, as it was, apart from the clothes I wore, my only possession.

The other matter which I would always attribute to Jean, because she was a snob, was that she believed I should go to the local grammar school and she insisted I work hard for the eleven-plus. I passed with ease and would have gone to Tynemouth but for a change in my fortune which was sadly not for the better.

Ray and Jean had wanted to adopt me and strangely enough I thought that would have been a good idea. I was not close to them, but they were kind and always seemed to look out for me. Looking back now, I wish I had been a better "son" to them. Every year they sent me birthday cards and although I did not know at the time, they enclosed a five-pound note. Years later, I did go to both of their funerals. This was out of character for me as I was almost a recluse. I did not do social events and I did not really grieve their deaths. Jean died in the spring and

Ray died some three months later. I had spoken to him at Jean's funeral and he told me he was not going to be around after the summer. He asked if I could say a few words at his funeral. I said that the idea filled me with dread and that I would rather be the corpse than the speaker, but I should be pleased to do so. I presumed it was just his grief talking. In the event, Ray did not see out the summer and I did say a few words at his funeral, but they were the hardest of my life. I was astonished when they left me everything in their wills.

The reason that I had not been adopted was because I had been reclaimed from Jean and Ray by a young woman, who I neither knew nor recognised, and it seemed she only needed me so she could apply for a council flat. On return to the woman who had given birth to me, there was no question as to which school I would go to. She had no aspirations for me like Jean had. I was simply enrolled in a school in inner city Newcastle, as it was convenient to where my "mother" lived. I was reacquainted with my aunts. All were disappointed to see me. The living conditions were already cramped and dirty and I just increased the numbers. The other difference was that now there were men about. One in particular seemed hostile. He always greeted me with a thump on the arm. He was called Eddie but I named him "Eddie the arm thumper" which I shortened to "Thumper". The girl who gave birth to me would chastise him in a flirty way when he thumped me. She would then turn to me, saying,

'He's only trying to toughen you up like a father would do.' I reverted to some long-remembered coping mechanism and started to say nothing. I found some of my aunt's speech was almost too hard to understand and when I did speak, I was mocked for having a posh Tynemouth accent. I could not believe that my time with Ray and Jean had had such an effect. I was a stranger with my blood family and could not even speak their language.

I did not fit in at school either; mainly because I was able to do everything asked of me and more. I was significantly cleverer than the woodwork master who stepped in to cover mathematics for a term. I was not trouble, but I knew that I was causing most of the teachers who had to teach me some discomfort. The lady who gave birth to me was summoned to the school. She came with Thumper, thank goodness – Thumper knew more about me than she did. Both assumed they were to hear what a problem I was and how my behaviour was to improve. On the contrary; the Headteacher wanted to get me special help as he thought I could get "O" levels. It would mean I would have a disrupted day and a changed curriculum. Thumper and Vera, as I begrudgingly began to call her, were mildly indifferent but I was pleased that someone seemed to care.

So, for two or so years, I was the strange boy who spoke posh and everyone assumed had to do extra lessons because he was thick. The girl who gave birth to me eventually got a flat, but it was not needed for long. Thumper was offered a security position with a private hospital on the outskirts of a North Yorkshire town. The new job came with a cottage; the downside was that Thumper lived above the shop so was always on duty. Vera was always angry with him as he was always working. I tried to keep out of her way as much as possible. Thumper used to struggle with his time sheets and rotas, so I helped him draw up co-ordinated tables and diaries. These proved to be so helpful that he was able to assist the other men that he worked with. It had other consequences too; one was that he had far more control of his time and so in theory, Vera would see more of him. The second was that he was given promotion and a pay rise so Vera was happy. Thirdly, Thumper was so grateful to me that he bought me a fishing rod. This was my second possession and was cherished as much as my Timex. Thumper loved the country and he and I became good friends. We would go fishing in a lake in the hospital grounds. We never caught anything, but we could fill hours saying nothing, just gazing at the water. As Thumper and I grew closer, he and Vera were growing further apart. I am not sure if the two changes were related but Vera upped and left one Friday. She said she was missing the bright lights. She did not ask me if I wanted to go with her or ask Thumper if he was able to keep me. It was the last time I saw her and I did not even care. Thumper was genuinely looking out for me and he seemed happy. We never discussed the change of circumstances. It was Thumper that arranged my grammar school interview. He took with him my logarithm tables. Thumper thought these were so complicated that I must be a genius. I had tried to explain calculus to him and he just hugged me. He said he wished he was my dad. As it turned out, and nothing to do with the logarithm tables, the school were impressed. I was offered a place and I started, without uniform, the following Monday.

Thumper was delighted and even more "chuffed" when everything to do with the school had me down as Peter Hardy. Hardy was his surname. We both thought it was fate and so I am still Hardy today, albeit most folk only ever know me as Geordie.

I never really had any friends before I arrived at my new grammar school. I spoke a different language and was always Geordie. There was the usual school bully, Ryan Haston, and he took against me on day one when I was in "home clothes" because I did not have my uniform. He called me "the great unwashed" and objected to the school letting poor folk in. He was probably half joking, but I had a chip on my shoulder, especially having memories of going back to the smelly family home. My mistake was telling Haston what I thought of him. None of his crowd, nor he, were interested in what I said. All just screeched at my accent and started to mimic me, as cruelly as schoolboys could. One chap came over and put his arm round my shoulder and walked me away from the taunts. His name was Shawcross. Shawcross grabbed me at the first rugby training and said, 'You will be one of the backs, come with me.' I later learnt that the forwards who trained separately on a Monday were going to "muller me in the scrum", for being rude to Haston. I had no idea what a scrum was, but understood the sentiments. I stuck with Shawcross whenever possible. I taught him maths and did most of his maths homework for him. Shawcross was always just there. Shawcross was not big or strong, far from it, but people respected his cool demeanour and listened to him.

Shawcross captained the rugby sevens side and even though rugby remained a dark art to me, I played in his team, because he asked. Haston was on the same side but by then we just simply ignored each other. I will never remember why, but in some competition against Eston Grammar School or someone, Haston and I had a fight. I suppose it was inevitable but what was more extraordinary was that on the following weekend he and I agreed to go with the team somewhere for a party. I had no idea about the geography of the area and had I known I should never have gone; it was miles away. I went because Shawcross asked me and I had never been asked to anything before. The party was in some flash fancy house. As we arrived at the end of the drive I said, 'Whey, warra manshun.' I had lapsed into my broadest

Geordie and the rest laughed at me in derision. It was good humoured and, for the first time in my life, I did not get angry. I smiled with them – even Haston.

I did love the music that was throbbing out of two huge speakers. It filled the room and made my heart beat to the speed of the drums. The music was being played by someone actually paid to play records at the party. He had every record you could imagine and he let me look at them and showed me how to play them on the two record decks. I was in heaven and lost in the music and magic. Over by the bar area, Haston and some of the host's friends were singing, drinking too much and getting noisy and boisterous. The DJ said, 'We can calm the room down with the music, that'll help.' He put on a slower Motown track and he was right. The whole room calmed down, save for Haston and his three stooges, who had apples in their mouths and were pretending to be pigs. I was not sure Haston needed the apple. Haston then grabbed an orange and, egged on by his group, proceeded to put it wholly in his mouth. Everyone was impressed and howling with drink-fuelled admiration. Haston had achieved his objective, as the room stopped to gawp at him. It was clear he could not get it out. His teeth were on the wrong side of the orange as it was fully in his mouth. He was clawing and gesticulating. He was going red and snorting through his nose. A couple of guys got him to his knees and tried to grab the orange, to no avail. Haston started collapsing and twitching. Everyone started screaming. I turned the music off and noticed that the DJ had gone to the phone in the hall.

Suddenly, Shawcross ran in. He was armed with a knife. He cut open the orange and pulled it out of Haston's mouth. He saved Haston's life, plain and simple. It was remarkable. What a hero. Everyone was so impressed, except the house owner who seemed to arrive just as the crisis was over. He wasted no time and threw us all out. The stuck-up lady of the house was telling Shawcross off. I tried to tell her she was kicking the wrong dog, but it only made matters worse.

I do remember spending a horrible night in a graveyard. My Timex had illuminated dials and I spent the whole night awake watching them slowly move. It was my comfort blanket. Shawcross slept on the outside of the group to protect us. I vowed that whatever happened to me in my life from then on, from that night forth I was going to look out for Shawcross. He deserved a medal. We gave Haston the nick name "Jaffa" after the orange, but typically, Haston was quite pleased. I had hoped he would have been embarrassed by it, like I would have been, but he was not.

## Attachment 3

## All property is theft

**Caroline Jervis**

The Old Vicarage in Corton was recorded as a dwelling in the Domesday Book and my father has a note, cutting and photo of every time it has been mentioned since. We have the deeds, the press cuttings, the plans, the maps, and a record of every activity since my parents purchased it in 1957, long before I was born. In the orangery that was added in the 1920s, or should I say completed on 1st April 1925, there is the garden chronicle, volume 11, which records all plants, trees and shrubs planted in the two-acre formal garden since the Victorian epoch. The book, leather bound, records the names of the gardeners and under-gardeners who have worked keeping it in show condition. Vicars were clearly wealthy, and the occupants of this old vicarage had to be. My parents were hostages to the house. In the early years it almost broke them as the mortgage was so expensive. Both were doctors and earning well, but it seems all their income was used to repair and renew. The building had been neglected for decades before being sold by the Church of England, as even they, one of the richest landowners in the country, could not afford the upkeep. When Mark was born, Mother stopped work, and half the household income went. He was going to be an only child so Mother could get back to earning funds to pay for the house, but I put the mockers on that, arriving some ten months after Mark. We did not have holidays; we had projects in the garden. We did not get a colour TV when every friend had one, we had the dry rot in the pantry sorted. Mark and I hated the house. Friends who came were always awestruck by the secret passage down through the cellar and off towards the church. It was my father's constant regret that he had not had the now blocked tunnel excavated to its full extent, but it did make a perfect wine cellar, so he was partially assuaged.

My parents were both of some vague Eastern European extraction, the name Jervis being a somewhat more anglicised name than the original. We never discussed the past and our heritage was supplanted by that of the house. The house made us middle class gentry, and whilst many of our parents' friends' children were sent away to school, Mark and I were schooled locally and then both went to grammar schools.

I only have one lasting memory of the house as a child. It was the night I met the man I was to eventually marry. I sort of knew he was special, but I never knew that a teenage longing could come true and after such a complex and quite extraordinary set of circumstances. My brother Mark developed a growth on his neck. It was first dismissed as a rugby injury, as he was getting pains and only felt comfortable if he held his neck at an angle.

Mother and Father were, of course, disinterested. They were doctors and we were not allowed to be sick. When the swelling started to grow, Mark was reluctantly dispatched to the local GP who, having carried out blood tests and that sort of thing, immediately had Mark admitted to the hospital in Newcastle. I only visited once but he was away for almost a month. The growth was removed and Mark took several months to recover. Father, in one of his weaker moments, said that Mark could have a party "when all this nonsense is over". The precious house "open" for a party! Mark's party. Father kept putting it off and it was clear that his excuses were becoming more and more fanciful. They were often based on his concern that Mark was not strong enough. When Mark declared that he was captaining his school rugby team in a tournament, he prevailed on my parents to set the date for the Saturday after the tournament.

It was agreed that Mother and Father would be out from 7 o'clock until 10 o'clock but on their return, if all was well, they would retire to their bedroom so the party could continue. During the planning, extra concessions were negotiated and after Mark returned victorious from the rugby and told Father he had invited the opposition, even this was accepted, albeit with thinly concealed annoyance.

It is when you are drafting invitations that you realise how few friends you have. I had lots of acquaintances and many passing strangers who had spent hours in my company at school, but I did not really know them. I settled on fifteen and Mark slightly more. The house could have accommodated so many more, but we agreed to close off two or three rooms. It was when thinking of this that Mark and I were surprised by just how many rooms we never even went into.

I first glimpsed the group of strangers arriving at the party as it was just as Mother and Father left. It looked like Father was going to speak to them, so I retreated. I did not want him to embarrass them with some lecture on behaviour. This was poignant, particularly when I think of what happened that night.

*When the ball was at its height, on that still and tropic night* – I still remember the words from the *Green-Eyed God* that I was learning as I went through the orangery following Jenny. Whenever Jenny came to the Old Vicarage, she would go into what she always called the "glass house". She would stand behind two of the large pot plants, she would open the palm fronds, whilst putting her head between them and she would say, 'Very interesting... but stupid!' I think this was from an American TV programme starring Goldie Hawn, but I never confirmed it with her. I thought I would beat her to it. I nipped in behind her and went behind the palms. When I peeled them back, it was Mark sitting in the lounger. He was startled and jumped up. It actually wasn't Mark, but one of the strangers. I did feel such an idiot, but he was kind and charming and I found myself sitting chatting to him.

I have no idea what we talked about. I was worried that I would say something stupid and he would see how shallow and immature I was.

Jenny asked if I was alright at some point, as did one or two others but I was so enchanted by this boy that I dismissed them. I was minded how anti-social I was, but reassured myself that it was Mark's party not mine and so he should be checking everything.

Then there were the screams and shouts. We jumped up. I did not even know my new friend's name at that point but followed him into the main party room. A man I did not recognise was choking and everyone was panicking, everyone that is, except my man. He grabbed a knife and effortlessly cut the obstruction which was a large orange from the victim's mouth. The room was so quiet, which made my parents' entrance "stage left" so poignant. Dad took control and even though it was premature, he stopped the party. It was such a shocking episode that everyone just seemed to pick up their coats and go. I so wanted to speak to my new friend, but Father and then Mother spoke to him and I did not get a chance. The ambulance took the idiot away.

The hero's friend said in a broad Geordie accent, 'It should have been to the psychiatric hospital in a straitjacket.' Mark missed everything. He had seemingly wandered off to "show Erica the orchard".

This did bring out some humour from Father, as he made some quip about leading Erica up the garden path.

Some days later, I mentioned to my father what had happened and tried to explain. My father stopped me and said that he knew. The young fellow who he put in the ambulance had explained everything to him. Father also told me that he "owed one young chap an apology, as his quick thinking and prompt action saved a life". Little did I know then that the apology would be given by the father of the bride at my wedding.

## Attachment 4

## Tabula Rasa

*"I have the brain of a genius – I keep it in a jar on my desk". The Tabula Rasa or blank state hypothesis is that people are born with no genetic, innate or evolutionary content. Rather, they are an empty disc onto which their life is written by experience, learning, example and their environment.*

*In the 1970s, eight "normal" healthy researchers gained access to American mental hospitals by reporting only one symptom; that "they were hearing voices". Once in the institutions, they behaved entirely normally. Seven were diagnosed as schizophrenic. When they "came clean" and admitted their guise, it took almost three weeks to get them released. Some time later, the same researchers told the same institutions that there were other "fake" patients trying to gain access. The result was that 19 genuine patients were suspected of fraud. The conclusion being that it is difficult to distinguish between the sane and insane.*

*In 1950, the famous codebreaker and mathematician Alan Turing came up with the "Turing test" for Artificial Intelligence: "a computer could be called intelligent if it could deceive a human into believing it was human". Big Blue, the IBM Computer, beat grandmasters to be a chess champion, but it was Parry that was the most successful.*

*Parry pretended to be paranoid and was questioned by a group of psychiatrists. The results were revealing: none of the group would believe that they were dealing with a computer, even when they were introduced to it. The transcripts were later mixed with genuine paranoid patients' records and sent to psychiatrists, none of whom could distinguish between the two.*

## Ryan Haston

Born clever and good-looking into a rich family is not necessarily a winning combination. I was a beautiful baby, so much so that my doting mother entered me for every "Bonny Baby" contest imaginable for the first four years of my life. As I grew, I became more photogenic. With the onset of television with adverts, I was always at film studios and shoots. Even at ten years old, my lasting memory is sitting in a caravan having make-up applied. I never really saw my father. He indulged my mother who had a fierce temper and always got her own way. I did not know then what hold Mother had over Father, save that her word was final. Of course, I know now. Father was a senior executive with ICI, the chemical giant. He had a driver and a mistress and whilst he kept Mother and me in splendour; it came at a price.

I should have gone to the prep school that my father went to and then on to Ampleforth, my father's *alma mater,* but Mother wouldn't let me out of her sight. I also earned a king's ransom from my film work and this allowed my mother to buy her independence. I would have been successful in Mother's eyes if I had become the "Milky Bar Kid". I did not.

I grew too quickly and grew too belligerent. I had all my mother's worst traits. I wanted my own way, and I started to resent sitting around whilst people faffed about, instead of taking a picture or filming a scene. I was never entered for drama classes or elocution. All I had was blond hair and chiselled cheek bones, and these were "features that most boys would die for". It was not me saying that, but one of the "trusted" photographers who used to look out for me when Mother was absent without leave. Frank, the said photographer, would stroke my cheek and say, 'This face will one day get you into so much trouble.' I did hear that some years later that it was stroking some boy's face that got him into trouble. I can say however, save as described, he never laid a finger on me. My star shine had tarnished by eleven. Mother had a mild stroke and lost some mobility. Father was working from Cheshire but this was a euphemism as he was really living in Chop Gate on a farm with Glenna.

I had almost a home school education until I passed my eleven-plus and was despatched to grammar school. I loved the structure of grammar school; rigid discipline and set timetables. A uniform, lunches at twelve thirty, double chemistry, cricket and rugby. Proper friends, proper teammates. People like me; all boys. No girls, no make-up, no dressing up and no faffing! I did get into some fights early on. Mother said that in the first few weeks of any new place you had to make your mark. Mother had a place at the Royal Ballet School when she was eleven or thereabouts. Sadly, as a young girl too far from home, she did not last a term. She was adamant it was because she let herself be bullied. She did stress that I should neither be a bully nor let anyone bully me. I followed Mother's advice to the letter.

When I started playing rugby, my father was delighted, and whilst I never sought his affection, I was so pleased. One day, as I was polishing my rugby boots, he expressed how happy he was that I was turning into a man, as he had always feared the worst. My father was to die of a massive heart attack several months before my announcement which, had he heard, would have brought on the attack earlier.

I do not look back with any ill-feeling towards the school. I was fond of my time there. I was caned five times. This was not a school record, only because no one kept them, but old Geoff Farnthwait thought it probably was. Once was for cricket. We were thrashed on the pitch at cricket and then again in old Geoff's office. My last thrashing was the most annoying. I was reported to the school for some high jinks at a party which landed me in hospital. In fact I wasn't reported as such, Shawcross was. He was my best friend. He was captain of rugby and everyone looked up to him, especially this rat Geordie. Geordie was always butting in and coming between Shawcross and me. We had a fight once on the rugby pitch in some competition. I think he was playing for the other side Rievaulx, we were Jervaulx. That cleared the air and I even persuaded him to come to a party that I had been invited to. I remember persuading Shawcross to join us and a couple of others.

The party was near Darlington. I do know that, because that was the hospital that they took me to after Shawcross saved my life. The party was in a fancy house owned by a friend of my father. Seemingly dad and the doctor played golf at Eaglescliff together and of course they were both Masons. Dad never knew how the doctor was allowed to join, as Dad believed he was Russian Orthodox or some other religion. Mind you, dad was not one to preach, he did not have any morals and did not follow any creed but his own. Dad wanted me to be a Lewis when I was old enough but I gave it a body swerve. A Lewis is both a Masonic symbol, (a prong to hold up a stone) and a young man adopted by the Lodge. My duty as a Lewis would have been to support the sinking powers and aid the failing strength of my father. He was as tough as old boots, so it was never going to happen in a Masonic nor a domestic fashion.

I do remember the trip to the party took forever. We argued all the way, but the warring stopped when we arrived. There was plenty to drink and I met up with the rugger buggers from the tournament. I was having a great time. I do not remember exactly what happened, but we were singing the usual rugby songs and doing the forfeits. Some fellow had to eat twelve sausage rolls and sing:

*Holes in his hands, holes in his feet, he could not juggle with a peanut treat…*
*has anybody seen JC; not since Easter Sunday, riding on a pony*

Gosh I can still remember the old songs.

*Second verse, same as the first, a little bit louder and a little bit worse*

I had to eat an orange in one go. I think the idea is that you remove the skin first, but I did not. I woke up in an ambulance with a sore jaw and under mild sedation. Seemingly I had had a fit and Shawcross saved my life. Father came over that night, having picked Mother up on the way. They stayed at some hotel and I was discharged on the Sunday. I had my bag and also the tent poles. I was never sure why they were with me on the ward.

I did not go back to school until the Wednesday. Mother said I needed a couple of days to get my strength back. By the Wednesday, the doctor, Mark's father, had spoken to the headmaster to praise Shawcross for his fast action and heroics. I did not come out of that conversation too well and so hence my fifth visit to Farnthwait for the stick. Everyone was calling me Jaffa. I was angry at first, but Mother said it would make me stand out, that all the famous stars had a stage name and I had to learn to embrace and enjoy the attention.

## Attachment 5
## Bland

*Whether you are eating in Palm Beach or Palma; Bognor or Bogotá, a McDonald's burger will taste just the same. People feel safe with things they understand; they like the comfort of predictability. The concept is not new. The Romans designed and built all their forts so, where possible, they were all exactly the same. It meant that a soldier arriving in Vindolanda or Palma at night always knew where to find his room but, more importantly, the position from where he could fight. If you were blindfolded and dropped into an "out of town" retail park, would you know where you were when you removed the eye covering? As you gazed at the row of Currys, Asda and Carpetright, would you realise you could be anywhere from Aldershot to Oldham? Everything, including the suburbs, is being brought down to the lowest common denominator. This extraordinary convergence applies to insurance companies, banks, TV programmes, politicians and chocolate bars; they are all becoming the same. The more people you try and please, the broader the appeal has to become. "Bland" would be a great name for a boy band, a pizza topping or a phone company.*

**Gordon Shawcross**

So here I was at thirty, Gordon Shawcross, working for an insurance underwriter. I was living in a flat in

Streatham; I was bland writ large. My only claim to fame was that I was captain of the squash club. I was not the best squash player, in fact I was one of the worst, so I had been surprised to be asked by the president to take on the role. I had asked, 'Why me?' and the president said, 'Because it is so unlikely anyone would object.' I had a flashback to the distant past and Chub Richards, that prescient school rugby coach.

There had been various girlfriends I had been fond of. In fact, I had been quite keen on one, but she was less fond of me. I established the desirability inverse square rule. The less I liked my "date", the more they liked me and vice versa. I had tried some reverse logic with one girl that I did rather like. I played a slightly diffident and aloof character on the date and unsurprisingly it ended with her telling me how rude I was. I tried to explain that it was because I fancied her so much that I was trying to be offhand, but this made me look even more of a scheming cad.

One Friday evening, I was literally kicking a can down Streatham High Road as I headed home from work. The first kick was an accident as the can was lying in the road and I had not noticed it, but the second and third were because I could. I did pick it up and put it in a bin eventually. The pubs were emptying out and the high street was busy. I was angry with myself as I had worked late dealing with a client in Singapore. The call to Asia had been such a waste of time and yet I had killed four hours waiting to make it and it had lasted four minutes.

As I approached my flat, I was stopped by a man who said, 'Thank God I have found you. I need help. I need it badly and I need it now.' It was unmistakably Haston. He had a beard, was walking with a stoop and carrying a kitbag. I was startled at first, but he almost laughed and I found him taking his kitbag and putting it across my shoulders. Nothing was said until we got back to the flat. I had a flatmate, but he was seldom home, preferring a girlfriend's company to mine, so the flat was empty.

I sat Haston down and went into the galley kitchen to make coffee and when I returned Haston was asleep on the sofa. I had no idea what to do, so I threw a blanket over him and drank my coffee. I tried to work out when I had last seen or heard of Haston and guessed it was 13-odd years ago. It was now past midnight and I decided that I needed some answers, so I shook him awake; he nodded and said, 'Loo?'. I gesticulated to a door, and he went through to the bathroom. He returned and flopped back down onto the sofa. The cup of cold coffee was in front of him and he picked it up and held it in two hands as if to reheat it. I offered to make him a fresh one, but he declined mouthed, 'Water'. I went through to the kitchen and filled a glass. When I gave it to him, he emptied it down his throat in one mouthful.

I must have said something like, 'Well, Jaffa Haston. It is good to see you. Why the mystery?' because he told me his name was no longer Haston.

He said, 'I am Cross.' He was struggling to speak and asked for another glass of water. I wondered if it was because of some drug he had taken. His lips were red and may have been swollen. He explained that he went to drama school and when he wanted his equity card, there was already a Haston so he became Cross.

I had no idea about stage names and remember asking about whether he kept his original name for real life.

He replied something about nobody would want his real life and he did not either. I found that we were being distracted by names. Haston explained that loads of people had different names and he had chosen Cross as a tribute to me for saving his life. Seemingly Hardy, another name from the past, wasn't originally called Hardy. Hardy had taken the name of his guardian.

I broke Haston's train of thought and asked him outright why he was on my sofa.

Haston started to ramble on about how nothing had ever gone as he planned. Life was miserable. Loads of hollow platitudes about misery that I thought he probably learnt at drama school. I had had a long day and was tetchy. His speech was getting worse. I did not want to provide a needy Haston with psychiatric support by letting him pour out his troubles whilst lying on my couch. I was reminded that Hardy once told me that Haston needed a psychiatrist; maybe he was right, even though that was a decade and a half ago.

I snapped at him by asking if he needed to borrow money.

He was at pains to stress he did not need money; what he needed was a couple of days' rest and some help recovering his portfolio. The portfolio contained all the lyrics for his new show.

I asked where the portfolio was and a more cogent tale emerged.

Haston was acting in a popular burlesque show in the West End. He was almost nocturnal and shared digs with friends where he hot-bunked. Seemingly, this meant he slept during the day and some other chap with a normal routine slept in the bunk at night. It sounded dreadful to me and it did to Haston. So, when he met a civil servant, who offered accommodation, he was pleased to accept. He had named the civil servant Humphrey after *Yes Minister*. Humphrey was married and went away to the family home at weekends and Haston looked after the empty flat in Chelsea at weekends. Haston did not elaborate what happened during the week. The problem was that he had fallen out with Humphrey. Haston had left a couple of nights earlier and wanted to collect his remaining possessions at the weekend when Humphrey was away. He asked me if I could be his courier and collect his portfolio. He did not want to bump into Humphrey and have another scene. I checked at the phrase "another scene".

I did not intend to step into the middle of Haston's domestic fight and told him I could not help.

Haston was adamant that Humphrey was an inoffensive gentleman and would be pleased that I had returned the keys to the flat and resolved this outstanding matter with such ease.

I asked why it had to be me and why not all of his actor friends from the West End. I told him that they could turn up as Michael Caine, Albert Steptoe, Ronnie Barker or even themselves, collect the folder and return the keys – job finished!

Haston explained that the portfolio was in the safe and he simply did not know one person that he could trust except for me. Sadly, I allowed the flattery to cloud my judgement. It was late and whilst it was no excuse, I was tired and more disturbingly, I had become so self-centred that I almost wanted to be wanted by someone, even if it was a scruffy Haston. I was also curious as to how Haston had found me.

I suggested to Haston that I may have been in Wormwood Scrubs for the last decade and may not be as trustworthy as Haston expected.

Haston scoffed and told me that I was easy to find. He had simply phoned the school and the secretary to the Old Boys' Association gave him my address. He told them that he was sending invitations to his 30th birthday. Haston asked for another glass of water. He smiled and told me he was suffering from the effects of a kebab sauce. We both laughed and I, for the first time since our meeting, relaxed.

I agreed to go to the flat first thing in the morning. I would pick up the portfolio, push the keys back through the letterbox and bring the portfolio back to Haston in Streatham. Haston wrote the safe code on a piece of paper, gave me the key and the address. He then hugged me.

I put Haston in my flatmate's room and just hoped he did not return that night or he was in for a shock. Haston said he would grab a shower and turn in. Next morning, I looked in on Haston who was crashed out on the bed fully clothed. I was surprised that he seemed to have redressed after his shower. I thought that might mean he needed to have a fast escape. I put any sinister thoughts out of my mind as I just assumed he had skipped the shower. He had said he needed rest and I am not sure why, but I thought best not to wake him.

So, Saturday morning, armed with an address, a key and a code number, I made my way to Chelsea. I had some misgivings about the mission, but was more annoyed that I could not find my razor and so had not shaved. I presumed that Haston had taken it to remove his beard. It was the last razor blade anyway, so I made a mental note to buy some. I did feel grimy, but I was anxious to get this errand out of the way. Embankment Gardens are down by Chelsea Embankment and so I had some walk from Sloane Square Underground Station. It was a beautiful area of London and with a cool breeze off the Thames, my spirits were lifted. I found the house easily and went down a short flight of stairs to the flat entrance. I knocked and waited before knocking again. It was just past 11 o'clock, so I assumed if anyone was in, they would be up and about. Two men walked past the house at street level above me and looked down. I smiled but they walked on. I did feel nervous as I turned the deadlock and then opened the door with the Yale key. I went in. It was small but beautifully furnished. It seemed so far removed from the hot bunk Haston had described, I realised why this would be an attractive proposition for Haston.

It was easy to find the large safe under the stairwell, which I presumed went up to the flat above. 27L81R49L, plenty of sevens there, I thought for some inexplicable reason. The safe opened and it was rammed with documents as well as a Rolex box, a wallet stuffed with large denomination notes and other envelopes and cheque books. There was a wrapped parcel on top of everything and I had to take it out to find the folder. I now understood why Haston would not have wanted anyone to open this safe. I noticed that there was a passport and when I opened it, there was a picture of Haston. I thought that Haston would need that too, so I put it in my pocket. There seemed to be a bundle of travel tickets and foreign currency and there was the locked folder which was just as Haston had described. The folder was bigger and thicker than I expected and bound in calf leather. It looked rather too good for Haston's portfolio, but then I remembered how rich Haston had been as a child. It was probably his father's case.

The cheque books were in the name of Anthony Stein and one of the letters was addressed to Mr A P Stein. I put the parcel back on the top of everything and closed the safe. I could not resist a sneaky look in the two bedrooms, more from curiosity than anything else. I was struck how impersonal the flat was. It was like a show flat. Not one photo nor one ornament. A beautiful flat in a beautiful setting and yet so sterile. Whoever lived here had thousands of books and all were neat and tidy and probably catalogued in accordance with a standard system of library classification. I had been asked to review my firm's library. I had become a bore on whether the layout was enumerative, hierarchical and faceted terms of functionality and so, clearly, was the owner of these books. There was an expensive Bang & Olufsen record deck in one corner and a beautiful chest, full of what seemed to be classical records. I looked in the bathroom and there was an open washbag on the shelf. I observed that this was the only thing out of place, as it suggested someone might even live in the flat. I was tempted to nick a couple of razor blades and that brought me back down to earth, and I decided that my task was complete.

I locked the flat and then, as instructed, poked the keys through the letterbox. As I climbed the stairs, I was greeted by the two men who had passed earlier. I remember saying 'Good morning,' but they didn't smile.

One said something to the effect of, 'Get in the car, Mr Shawcross.' The second man took the folder from under my arm. I did not resist. It was the silence that disturbed me. Neither man spoke after that.

I asked who they were and where they were taking me, but silently, I was eased into the back seat of a black car. I muttered that I had nothing to hide and could explain everything. Nothing was said. We drove in silence for twenty minutes or so. It appeared to be the Pimlico area. I was released from the car and ushered into a red brick house. It had netting on the windows. I had read that all government buildings had them installed after the Harrods bomb to stop glass shattering. I was surprised how calm I felt. I had just taken items unknown from a safe in a flat owned by a stranger at the request of someone I had not seen for over a decade. I could not understand why I was not panicking. I felt my pulse to see if it was racing; it was not. I had for some reason, probably guilt, assumed that I would be taken to a police station, but this was a normal London house. I was shown into what appeared to be the study or library, as it had thousands of books. Unbidden, I was given a cup of tea and a custard cream by one of the men that had accompanied me to the house.

A lady came in. She was a similar age to me, but had her hair tied tightly back in a bun and this, together with her tweed suit and sensible shoes, made her look so much older.

'Sorry for interrupting your journey, but as you know, this should only take the time it takes you to enjoy your tea and biscuit.' I was about to speak, but she left the room. When she returned, she seemed agitated. 'Where is the parcel?' she enquired.

I told her that there must have been some misunderstanding

and I had no idea who she was, where I was and more importantly why I was sitting in her library drinking tea?

The lady's face flushed, and she said something about me committing treason and there still being a death penalty, but it being more usual to receive a long prison sentence.

I laughed. It was the death penalty threat that was simply unbelievable. It was the first of April; *I had been well and truly spoofed by Haston. These were his actor friends. It was "thank you" time.* I jumped up and said, 'Brilliant.' I found myself punching the air in a most uncharacteristic manner. 'Gosh, that was good, where is he? Where is Haston?'

The lady looked perplexed and she was re-joined by one of the men from the car who asked her if everything was alright.

'This is an April fool, isn't it?'

The man left the room as I was bidden to sit down by the lady, who continued to mutter about how serious the situation was. No one was laughing but me. It was not the 1st of April.

My accuser then launched into a steely analysis of the situation.
'Mr Cross, this is serious and you know it. This

morning you broke into a flat and stole documents, the disclosure of which could undermine the security of the realm. We are aware of your relationship with the flat owner. We are aware of the blackmail threats. What we are not aware of, is what you intend to do with the information when you get to Germany and, more importantly, to whom you intend to sell it. If you fully co-operate and we are satisfied you can help us with the answers to our questions, we can assist you. If you do not, we will simply hand you over to a less sympathetic agency.'

'Agency? Well, who are you?' I asked. I had misjudged the situation and felt uncomfortable. This was no joke; I had no idea what to say. I knew I had done nothing wrong, but I felt an overwhelming sense of shame and guilt. I felt slightly faint and had a sensation of wanting to cry. My pulse rate was quickening but I tried to remain in control. Almost counter-intuitively, I took a sip of tea and a bite of a biscuit. I felt calmer immediately and felt the blood returning to my brain. 'You called me Cross on two occasions. My name is Shawcross, Gordon Shawcross, but I presume you want my name, rank and number?'

'No, you are Sean Cross. Mr Sean Cross.'

'I know who I am!' I said indignantly, whilst trying to gather my faculties.

'You had keys to the flat,' she stated.

'You said I broke in and stole, so you clearly have no idea of what is going on,' I replied. 'Either let me walk out of here or call me a lawyer.' I was gaining in confidence as the lady seemed to be wavering. I was mindful that by taking the initiative, I was becoming more alert. I relaxed and smiled at my accuser and tried to think of what I could say. I smiled when I thought that all the years of watching *The Bill* and how it had prepared me for this moment.

The tweed lady was unsettled by the fact that I had relaxed and was smiling. I was asked if I had any other documents or papers from the Embankment Gardens flat other than the folder.

'Only this passport,' I had relaxed too much and bit my lip. *Why had I disclosed that I had the passport? Why was I so honest?* I handed over the passport I had collected that morning. She opened it, it had a picture of Haston, the name said "Sean Cross". I said, 'It isn't mine.'

'So you are not Sean Cross?' I was shocked that not only had Haston used "Cross" but had failed to mention the "Sean". Haston really had almost stolen my identity. A man stepped from behind me. It was neither of the men who had picked me up, but a smaller man in black glasses. He took the passport off me and passed it to the lady with the back open, showing the photograph. I saw him shake his head as he took it from her.

'Where is Mr Cross? Why have you taken his folder and passport?' I could feel the disappointment in the room. Shawcross was not who they wanted and Shawcross did not have whatever they were looking for. They wanted Sean Cross and he was sleeping in my spare room.

'Who are you?' I asked. 'Is this a normal Saturday in London for you, picking men up off the street, bundling them into cars and then subjecting them to an interrogation?' I was somewhat sharpened up by my knowledge that I was not who they wanted. I continued by giving them my address and phone number and telling them if they had anything further to ask, they could do so by appointment. I stood up. Nothing was said.

The man with the glasses ushered me out of the room and into the hall saying, 'You are free to go sir.'

I did protest, growling that I had no idea where I was and I needed the passport and folder.

The man smiled. 'I don't think so. You were in the wrong place at the wrong time, but don't push your luck.'

'But who are you?' I remonstrated, but it was to no

avail, as I was ejected into the street.

I had been right; I was in Pimlico, in Johnson's Place, near a church hall. The church had a fête in progress and people were crowding about the entrance. I mingled with them and watched the house where I had been held captive. I was bemused by the situation and noted that I was even thinking in emotive language. *Held captive.* After about ten minutes, the man who took me into the house and the lady with the tied-back hair came out and at the same time, the car that had been used to deliver me to the house pulled up and they climbed in. I would have loved to give chase or find out who they were or where they were going, but I just noted the number plate, model, and colour. I had no idea what I was doing it for, but felt it was what one does after being kidnapped. I was minded to wait to see if the man in glasses came out, but I was not sure what I would do if he did.

I returned empty-handed to an empty flat. Haston was gone and so had his kitbag. There was a note in red pen saying:

*Dear Shawcross,*

*Thank you for saving my skin. As usual, much ado about nothing, I have been as "civil as an orange". I will explain.*

*Jaffa*

I was not sure how to feel. I was not angry because I

tell myself it is such a wasted emotion but yes, I was wound up. *Maybe they had been back to the flat and picked Haston up*, I thought. I do confess that up to this incident, I had been feeling melancholic, I had been feeling bland and suddenly, like a Raymond Chandler novel, someone had burst in with the equivalent of a gun. I had, for a moment, been touched by something exciting. There was an adrenaline surge and I felt high. After circling my flat for the twentieth time, I went out onto Streatham High Street. *Where would Haston have gone?* I thought. On a whim, I decided to head to the West End and check out what Haston had called a burlesque show.

Even though I had lived in London for almost four years, I was still out of my depth in the capital. I was a Yorkshire lad and even four years at University in Uxbridge had not really prepared me for London life. The West End was another world. I had seen some shows and recognised Shaftesbury Avenue, but I was soon lost in the back streets. I was pleased it was six o'clock in the evening, as I felt uncomfortable and would not wish to have been in the area much later. I called in at several venues and asked if they were "burlesque" and received mixed receptions. I wasn't actually sure what "burlesque" was and that didn't help.

A striking young girl in the entrance to the Capital Theatre proved to be the most helpful. She explained it meant mockery in French. She waved her body as she demonstrated that it is "A provocative and comedic show with female choruses". She wanted to know why I was interested.

I said I was writing a book on theatre form.

The girl groaned, 'What rubbish – what is the real reason?' and so I found myself relating what had actually happened. The girl laughed so loudly.

The more I explained, the more absurd the story sounded and the more she laughed.

'Oh sorry, you are such a story teller. Please let me have your name if it is not James Bond, so I can buy the book.'

I chuckled and for effect said, 'Sean Cross.'

'No you are not. I know Sean,' was the sharp retort.

I forced a smile and, on the defensive, blurted out, 'Yes, he is a good friend of mine too.'

'Well, he is no friend of mine, he swanned off owing a month's rent. He then rocks up last week like nothing has happened and gives me a hug and money and takes his bike and boxes back.' She seemed so animated, that I was unsure what to say.

I ended up asking her rather lamely if she knew where he lived now or if she knew where he worked.

'So he owes you money as well, does he?' She told me that Cross had been a good tenant but had "done a moonlit flit". He had told her he was being put under pressure by people and he had to go to ground. She thought he may have been sharing a house above Madam YoJo's.

I apologised to her and gave her my correct name. She relaxed, smiled, and told me she was Lela. I gave Lela my number and she gave me hers. She offered to accompany me to the burlesque if I ever wanted to go. I said it would be something to look forward to. After directing me to Madam YoJo's, Lela bade farewell and gave me a warm kiss and a hug. It seemed so long since I had female company.

Madam YoJo's was not hard to find, but at 7 o'clock it was closed and there did not seem to be any flat above or to the sides that were accessible. I tried hanging about but felt far too self-conscious, so I went home.

When I had related the story to Lela, she laughed out loud. She was right, it was far-fetched. I had absolutely no evidence that Haston had even been with me, apart from the note. It was clear he had pinched my surname to give himself a new name. I sat down with a pen and then thought, *no, I will do this on my new computer*. It had been built for me by Martin Clegg, one of my work colleagues, who had a sideline in building personal computers. Until this sudden change in fortune, the new PC was proving my only challenge. It had a note book word processor facility and so I used the programme to list what I knew. It would take far longer than my pen and paper, but it gave me time to think.

Haston had met me in the street. He had a kitbag and was wearing a baggy coat over denim trousers. He had a T-shirt with a band's logo on the front and tour dates on the back. He talked of burlesque and having been to drama school. I remembered something about Haston saying he was a polyglot. I grabbed my dictionary off the shelf – so he spoke several languages. Nothing seemed helpful and then I got it. I would reverse engineer the way Haston found my Streatham address. I would phone the Old Boys' secretary and find Haston's address. *Eureka!* Whilst recording this on the screen, it froze. I did not re-boot, I had the thread I was seeking.

I had to wait until mid-morning on the Monday to telephone my old school. The school bursar's secretary doubled up as secretary to the Old Boys' Association. She was delighted to chat to me, as my star quality was that I re-joined the Old Boys every year and paid immediately. I explained that I had been invited to Haston's birthday party but had lost the invitation and needed to reply.

She advised me that this was no problem, except Haston had moved and so he had asked for his old address to be removed. Mrs Alexander no longer had it.

I asked her how she would be able to contact Haston in the future.

'Through Mr Hardy,' she replied.

I wrote down Hardy's address and thanked her. *What next?* I wondered.

## Attachment 6

## Danger

**Ryan Haston**

When I left school, I had a year out. Mother needed help, as she had had a second stroke. The doctor told me she would not make old bones. I joined the Hutton Players, the village amateur dramatic society and we put on *The Pirates of Penzance* in the village hall. I played Frederick and received rave reviews in the *Evening Gazette*. It nudged me into going to York University to read modern languages and Russian. Well, the review hardly nudged me, if the truth be known. The director of the show had been offered a lectureship in modern languages at York and was starting in the October. I did like him, but never saw him once in my five years at university. I had my father's financial backing and my mother's blessing. She died before I went up and it was helpful, as it meant I did not have to worry about her. The extra money also meant I could stay on and do my master's for two years. I only did this to stay in York and because there was nothing else I wanted to do. I was listless and lacked any motivation.

I had never been to any of the countless "milk rounds" that came to the university and I have no idea why I went to one whilst writing up my thesis. I was drawn to the "Government Services" kiosk. I had never dreamt there were so many interesting jobs in government and I am not being ironic. I was lined up for an interview in York, which I sailed through. I did some written tests, which seemed straightforward, and then had a second interview in London. This did not go so well, but through no fault of my own, the train broke down between Peterborough and King's Cross. I was anxious, as the interview was at 3 o'clock and I was meant to be in London for 1 o'clock. In the event, I arrived at the station at three thirty. I took a taxi to the address on the paper. I arrived almost 70 minutes late. The team of three that I faced were unconcerned, they said they knew the train was late. They knew everything about me. At one point, we all four chatted in Russian about the growing unrest in Poland.

After what seemed an inordinately long interview, the lead questioner said, 'Do you know who we are?' I expressed some vague answer that included government. They told me they were the Security Service.

I was dumbstruck and muttered, 'What, spies?' They all smiled.

'If we were to offer you training and development, do you think you would join us?' They said it would mean a short period without seeing friends and having some "freedoms" restricted, but in the most part, was a normal government job.

I said I would have to think about it, as I had hoped to spend a year at drama school. I am never sure why I told them that, as it had not crossed my mind until that moment.

I did not join them, or to be correct, I should say I did not realise that I had joined them. I was offered a "government job" in the department of technology at a research facility in Cambridge. I always assumed I received this offer because I had passed everything and even though I was not secret agent material, I was still employable in other government departments. I did take that job, as it turned out and then in the following October went to LAMDA, the oldest drama school in England. I was to be in Hammersmith for a year to do a one-year diploma. After I graduated, I did a series of small parts that were connected to the LAMDA outreach programme whilst I waited for my big break to come. It did not. I was asked to join a touring Shakespeare company on a trip to Latvia and Estonia. At the time, I was delighted that my talent had been noticed when so many of my better contemporaries were overlooked. There were five plays to rehearse and perform throughout the four-week tour. I never played any main part. I was always at the back of the fight in *Romeo and Juliet*. The only part where I actually had to act was as the porter in Macbeth. It seemed to me that I was there to make up the numbers. I was asked by the administrator of the troupe to assist with much of the negotiations when we were in

Riga and later Tallin. My chance to use my Russian made me quite enthusiastic about that role.

In Estonia I found that I was spending more time in strange meetings and discussing technical export and import issues than I was acting. It was one night when I was asked to pick up a student from Neeme, a coastal town, some 40 km from Tallin, that I paused to think. Robert, the administrator, was always once removed from the troupe. Robert was more like a school teacher than a tour manager. He had a small head and wore spectacles that seemed too large so they dominated his face; but most annoying was that he had absolutely no knowledge of Shakespeare. I would try and get a quote into the conversations with him at every opportunity, and he never once noticed, no matter how crass or obvious they were. On my way to Neeme, I realised that I was being used. I could not categorically say how, as it was all so subtle. I had not said no to anything but likewise, there had been no consent. The girl I collected was a ballerina called Marta. She spoke better English than I did, so I had not been needed for my Russian. I had to be discreet, seemingly because her father did not wish her to study abroad. Everything went well with the pick-up and trip back to re-join the troupe. When I confronted Robert as to why I had been sent on this meaningless task, he was quite dismissive. I was not rude or belligerent but expressed my disquiet.

He nodded and fiddled with his glasses. I could see he was uncomfortable. He responded, 'We will chat back in Blighty.'

Whilst the trip had been good for my CV, it had not improved my acting. I was not good at auditions. My work was drying up and, without my inheritance, I would have been waiting on tables, like so many of my profession. It was around this low point several months after my trip to the Baltic states that I was doorstepped by Robert. He said he had an acting role that needed a leading man like no other and it would be perfect for my skill set. He took me to a coffee shop in Denmark Street which was full of gay men. He asked if I was comfortable with homosexuals.

I said I had no problem and that acting and the arts was full of them. I was familiar with the area, but tended to avoid it, as it was always so crowded. The whole of Soho was reeling from the impact of AIDS and it was still being associated with the gay community, even though everyone was vulnerable.

Robert said, 'Thank you for your help during the Baltic trip. There is something else we need your help with.' He took off his glasses and looked me in the eye and said deliberately, 'Start listening – these are your lines and stage directions. We need you to meet a man who is a regular at the Bohemian burlesque show. You start working there on Friday week. You will be well looked after and there will be a pension in it for you, unless you do something stupid.' As the two coffees were delivered to the table, he pushed over a wallet full of money.

'There is a photo in the wallet of Mr Anthony Stein. He will probably be known as AP. He is not a big drinker and shuns any publicity. He has a strange interest in burlesque and cabaret clubs. Do use your discretion – no dramatics. You have a room organised from tonight. The key is in the pouch and the address is the one on the treasury tag. Just up and leave where you are. This whole thing could all be over before you learn your act or it could take longer, we will see how it goes. Use your current equity card name but be prepared to revert to Haston if we advise you. We will have your back. Mr Stein is harmless but we think he has interesting friends. Steve, the Manager, is expecting you. I hope you can sing.'

I had not agreed to anything but found myself grinning and listening, two traits that did not come easily.

'Any questions?' he asked.

'Well, yes', I said. 'What do I do when I get to know Mr Stein?' Robert smiled and put his glasses back on saying,

*Let me have men about me that are fat,*
*Sleek-headed men and such as sleep o' nights*
*Yond Cassius has a lean and hungry look;*
*He thinks too much; such men are dangerous.*

He stood up and winked at me. As he walked away, I shouted,

*The path is smooth that leadeth to danger.*

## Attachment 7

## Programming

Dulce et decorum est pro patria mori. *It is glorious and honourable to die for one's country. One hundred years ago, Eton had over 30 teachers of Latin and Classics but only one for science and one for maths. Schoolboys – there were, of course, no schoolgirls – could read and write Latin and could recite Horace from memory. Education was seen as a means of instilling morals and improving character. Some four years later, many of the same schoolboys were dying for their country, in the fields of Flanders. Whilst Latin is now of minor importance and we are teaching skills for the future, we forget the lessons of the past at our peril. Perhaps honour, dignity, self-discipline, integrity and modesty should be more prominent on the curriculum. Maybe employers should put greater emphasis on the quality of the candidate's character, not the quantity of qualifications.*

*The Senate in Rome always sent a man to the River Tiber to meet generals returning to the city after a military victory. The man's task was to stand in the chariot next to the general and remind the general "thou art but a man". Romans believed that success went straight to a man's head. Perhaps modesty is a trait that is now forgotten and has resulted in the excesses of some of our Members of Parliament, professional footballers, and corporate bankers. Benjamin Franklin noted that "Success has ruined many a man".*

*As citizens, taxpayers, shareholders, voters and parents, we should be looking more closely at those in positions of power, particularly the politicians, the captains of industry, the leaders of public companies and boards of utilities and quangos, to establish how they have dealt with "success". These leaders seldom spend or risk their own money and yet often receive disproportionate rewards.*

The higher my rank, the more humbly I behave. The greater my power, the less I exercise it. The richer my wealth, the more I give away. Thus, I avoid, respectively, envy and spite and misery. *(Sun Shu Ao, Chinese minister, c 600 BC).*

## Geordie Hardy

I was a rampant socialist by the time I went to polytechnic. My maths was such a high standard that I was offered places at Oxford, Cambridge, Durham and Edinburgh. My school pleaded with me to go, mainly out of self-interest as they wanted my name on the Oxbridge honours board. But I went to read computer science at Teesside Polytechnic. It did, strangely enough, have a good reputation and had its own mainframe, albeit in those days we were programming in Basic, Cobol and Fortran. My non-maths passion was music. I started as the polytechnic DJ in the Buttery and moved on to a club in the town which was always full of students. I still lived with Thumper but he had lost the original house when he was made redundant and so we had moved to a council house in Berwick Hills. Beverly Hills it was not. It was a rough neighbourhood, but it was perfect for my socialist ideals. My problem was that I could not help being enterprising and as I spent very little, lived at home and also had a student grant, I kept making good money as a DJ, which just accumulated.

During one of the general elections, I offered to help the Socialist candidate. He would go on to win by a landslide in Middlesbrough so I did not need to do much, and he could do even less. He was a barrister by profession and lived in London. For the six weeks of the campaign, he took three rooms in the Dragonara Hotel in central Middlesbrough. I became his trusty lieutenant. I could stay over in the operations room when I was having a late night following an evening event. Notwithstanding my political persuasion, I did enjoy the high life. The hotel had a casino and as a guest, I was given a membership card. The card was for a year and long after the election was won, I used the casino. I did not actually gamble much at first, but it was the perfect evening out, especially if your passion was maths and you could analyse the odds. You had to pay for alcohol, but soft drinks were free and, more importantly, they had a constant flow of free food. I was a regular, I always dressed smartly and I was on first names terms with all the croupiers and the manager. They all assumed I was related to the MP and so were always attentive. I did not have any close friends. Even at the Socialist Worker Society, I felt like an outsider. I was not a natural talker. I did have some dark moments but, thanks largely to Thumper, I pulled through. I was self-conscious of my Geordie accent and woeful in the presence of a female. I would stutter and blush, even talking computer language to Joy, who was the only female in my tutorial group.

One Friday evening I was having fish, chips, and mushy peas with Thumper. It was almost a ritual when I was not out running a disco. He asked me why, as a student surrounded by "lovely lasses", I did not have a girlfriend. I found myself crying and pouring my heart out to him and explained my insecurities. A man who I had adopted as my father proved to be remarkably sensitive to my issue and had the solution.

I had once shown and explained to Thumper the Perspex computer template ruler that I used to help me when writing a computer programme. He made me get the ruler and draw him the actions and write the code so the computer would work out the procedures for a date and the consequences. I wrote the programme. I had dialogue boxes for yes and no; it started something like this:

Line 1 Let Girl = X
Line 2 I like X yes:no
Line 3 If yes, ask her out
Line 4 If no, go back to line 1 choose next value for X
Line 5 If yes, proceed to date

It was all so simple when written as code.

So, I asked Joy, as the only girl who I ever had any contact with, if she wanted to come to the casino. I know she thought I was the nerd above all nerds, but strangely, she said that she would love to go to the casino. It was not quite a date, more that she accompanied me, as she had never been to a casino before. The casino was the attraction. It was a Thursday and quiet, but it meant that Joy and I had almost VIP treatment and everyone was friendly to "Mr Hardy". As a mathematician, I understood odds and chance, and so even though I never lost more than the £5 limit I would set myself, when I won, I could win big. Whether it was the presence of Joy who held my arm at the roulette wheel, or my pleasure that the dating programme worked, I do not know, but on that evening, I won £230. I insisted that Joy took £115, being half. She was staggered and as we walked back to her student house, she joked that she could never believe that she could have had the best night of her life with the most boring man she had ever met. It may have been a joke to Joy, but the sentiment bit hard into my deep insecurities. I would like to say that Joy and I found true love, but we did not. Joy did say that she was so troubled on the walk back to her student house that she almost cried. It was the money; she thought I would expect her to sleep with me, and she did not know how she would respond if I asked! Little did she realise that her company had been a first for me and nothing else was on my radar. It did however make me aware of the power of money in a manner that had never occurred to me before.

It was with Thumper's encouragement that we had to test the programme again to make sure it was robust. This proved so much easier than I had anticipated. Joy told all six girls in her student house about this computer whiz-kid who led a high-roller lifestyle. The six must have told another six and within a week or two there was not a girl on campus who did not want to come to the casino. Whilst they wanted to go, none showed any enthusiasm for me. The other downside was that my socialist credentials were being exposed as a sham. The Socialist Worker student society summoned me before a special committee to challenge my commitment to the cause. They had heard a corrupted story about my regular attendance at the casino and someone had suggested, I presume jokingly, that I had shares in the hotel group. They were all so earnest and self-righteous. I was pleased to tell them they were actually right.

I had been dabbling in the stock market. It was just gambling in a different form. I used to study *The*

*Financial Times* in the polytechnic library and had written a programme with my tutor to identify when a stock was falling below a certain level and do the same when stock was rising. On the corner of Albert Road there was a stockbroker and even though there was some initial embarrassment (for them) when they challenged why a poor Geordie student would want to trade stock, I was soon a regular. So back at the Socialist Society kangaroo court, I was able to say, 'Yes, I do believe I own shares – I will check my portfolio.' The Club voted to expel me and it was the start of my conversion to capitalism. None of the subsequent dates lived up to my "Joy moment", but most girls who put up with me earned a reasonable payout from the croupier and I had the company that I craved.

I was halfway through my final year when Jean and then Ray died, some three months apart. To my great surprise, I was their heir and inherited their house in Whitley Bay and over £20,000. I had been a shrewd saver whilst at college as a DJ, playing the tables and playing the stock market. I was able to move to London, buy a flat in Albert Mansions, just over Waterloo Bridge, and start work for a software company. The two young Americans who owned it were brilliant computer engineers but hopeless with budgets and finance and within three years they were working for me. I had meant, over the years, to find out what happened to Shawcross, but work got in the way. I had always considered Shawcross my only friend at school and whilst he may have saved Haston's life at the party, he, along with Thumper, had probably saved mine. That probably sounds a little too melodramatic, as I had been well supported by Mark Jervis and others. Mark was the one person from my school days I was in contact with and he had not even been at my school. When I decided to be a DJ in the Buttery, I needed some guidance and was desperate to speak to the DJ from the orange party. I rang the Jervises' house and Mark put me in touch with the DJ. It was the start of a regular chat with Mark and when I was at my loneliest, during the early polytechnic years, Mark was always happy to cheer me up. He went up to Oxford to read law and then came to a city firm. We still meet occasionally. He has been brilliant legal support and helped me enormously when I needed lawyers for my company buy-out. He also arranged the protection for my software that we are now selling to the London banks and trading houses. I went to his wedding when he married Francesca.

In fact, it was at his wedding that I met Sheena. Of course, I should not have met anyone. I did have those "dates" after Joy, but I could not communicate. I may have had a great venue to take a girl to, but I still did not have a personality and I was not interesting. I had asked Mark what I should wear to his wedding and he told me that everyone would be in morning suits and I should hire one if I did not own one. I liked the idea of owning one and so I booked an appointment in Savile Row and was fitted for a new tailcoat and waistcoat. I had never worn formal wear before and had certainly never been to a tailor. The whole experience was bizarre. The idea of standing in a plush room with a couple of men measuring me up and then choosing from ten shades of black was unthinkable for me; one of Haston's "great unwashed". I did not care that I would probably never wear the outfit again. I was not short of money and I loved the whole experience. I was so pleased with myself with the thought of a new outfit; I walked down to Jermyn Street where, on the advice of the tailor, I had some shoes made to measure.

Whilst the shoemaker measured my feet, he explained the process that would take place to make sure I was shod in the most comfortable shoes.

I accidently called him a cobbler and he feigned offence, explaining to me that a cobbler repaired shoes.

Whilst chatting, I explained how I lived in a digital world and his retort was that he still lived and worked in an analogue world.

He showed me what he called his closest friend. He lifted his hand and exposed a Cartier Santos watch on his wrist. He must have thought I was crazy as my eyes welled up as I thought of my old Timex. I had not worn it for a decade, but it was still my closest friend. On leaving the shoemaker, I went to a shop in Burlington Arcade and bought a Rolex watch. I had spent more in one morning than I had spent in the rest of my life.

I went to the wedding because I was invited and apart from work related matters, I still never received social invitations. It was going to be an uncomfortable event for me, but I had planned an early exit strategy. I had arranged, through one of the staff at work, a car with a driver. I was uncomfortable with taxis, another of my strange insecurities, as I thought taxis were for rich folk. I also thought I could escape on my terms, rather than be beholden to the timings of a normal taxi. The church was off Brompton Road. The car arrived earlier than I needed so I sat chatting to the driver outside my flat to kill some time.

The driver kept calling me "sir", which was unsettling, and he commented on how smartly I was turned out. He said he had been a Coldstream Guardsman and could always spot a proper gentleman. He asked if I had forgotten my buttonhole.

I confessed in my best southern Geordie accent, the accent where I try to sharpen my vowels, that I had no idea what a buttonhole was and that the handle of "sir" did not apply to me.

The driver replied, 'It only took the medal to make the lion brave in *The Wizard of Oz*. All you will need is a buttonhole.' So we went to the wedding via a florist.

I had warned the driver that I was planning a fast exit and gave him a likely pick-up time.

He said, 'Don't you worry, sir, I will be there exactly when you need me.'

As I left the car, I said, 'Is there anything else I should know?'

'Perhaps you should undo the bottom button of the waistcoat,' he replied.

All of the ushers, and there seemed to be a score of them, had tailcoats and all had the bottom button of their waistcoats undone. I presumed it was something you were taught at public school. I sat at the back of the church and watched the selection of fancy hats parade past. It seemed that the bigger the hat, the nearer the front its wearer was positioned by the officious ushers. Judging by the thickness of the order of service, which was in French and English, it was going to be a long service. I occupied my mind by counting the hats and working out the percentages of each colour.

The post-service photographs seemed to take forever. I

was, however, pleasantly surprised by how comfortable my feet felt in my handmade shoes. I was dividing their cost by the time I had worn them when I was startled by an usher. He almost manhandled me down towards the bride and groom. Seemingly I was missing from the "friends of the groom" photo. I received a short rebuke from Mark. He made some remark about me being more interested in my feet than the bride. I am sure the photo will show me with a red face after the scolding. I was pleased to escape to my car for the short trip to the reception. Save for a nod, I did not speak to my driver. He sensed my discomfort and produced a banana and a small bottle of water. He told me to line my stomach and rehydrate and I would be ready face the "hard part". He had a hip flask but I declined and he told me that that was the sensible option.

The reception was in a ballroom of a livery company in the city. I want to say the Grocers' Hall, but I was not paying much attention as I was fascinated by the beautiful entrance doors and lampshades hanging from the ceiling.

I had been to a couple of "normal" weddings of work colleagues, but this was the first that was "society". Everyone was from central casting. The father of the bride delivered a beautiful speech in English, pausing after each paragraph to repeat in French. This was adopted by the groom and the best man. I realised just how clever some people were. I would have struggled in English. I could see Mark's father and mother sitting on the top table. Mark's mother had told me off at the orange party and so I still had this strange fear of meeting her again. I have no idea why as she looked so benign and elegant in her green suit and large green hat. I was seated between Mark's accountant and a friend of Mark from Oxford. I was my usual boring self and whilst I was happy to chat about accountancy with the accountant, he was not. Hardly surprising. I had spent a disproportionate time playing with my fancy new Rolex as a distraction and trying to decide how early I could escape. I do not recall the order much but there was a comfort break after the speeches before they brought out coffee. I took the opportunity to walk and stand under the lampshade to get a better look before sneaking out.

'A rhombicosidodecahedron,' a voice beside me whispered.

I replied, '20 triangle faces, 30 square faces, 60 vertices and 120 edges.'

'But could you write down the Schläfli symbols?' she asked.

'But only if you do the symmetry group and rotation group.' *I was in conversation with a girl who spoke my language!* To this day, I cannot recall what she was wearing nor the size and colour of her hat. We went back to my table for the coffee and she sat where the accountant had sat and we discussed Johannes Kepler, Archimedean shapes, and dual icosidodecahedrons. Our napkins were covered in what must have been hieroglyphics to anyone looking and quite a few did.

At some point, a waiter coughed and said, 'Sir, we are inviting those still in the ballroom to move through to the garden room whist we prepare for this evening.' I looked round and it was only Sheena and I left. We both laughed and went through to join the rest of the guests. Sheena lived in Shoreditch but was happy to share my car home. She had no idea I lived in the opposite direction and assumed I was driving myself. Sheena was a proper guest and understood all the protocol that must be adopted before you can just up and leave a wedding. I had no idea about these dark arts so just followed her nodding at the appropriate times and maintaining a rictus grin.

Mrs Jervis, Mark's mother, rather than the new Mrs Jervis, the bride, was wearing pistachio, not green, seemingly. I just smiled when corrected. Sheena had said that when thanking the bride's mother, you have to say how good she looked. I had assumed that "I like your green frock" would have been appropriate; it was not. Thankfully, I knew I need never meet Mark's mother again.

Sheena was at the wedding with a friend, so the

mathematical discourse ended in the car. I became more self-conscious and worried that I would lapse into incomprehensible stuttering Geordie. I could feel myself sweating and breathing harder. Joe, the driver, lightened the mood by joking that we should all remove our shoes and relax. He told me to slacken my tie and smile as I was over the worst. I did and it worked I relaxed. The driver who had seen that I was engaged when he came to collect me some three hours earlier, was a shrewd judge of the situation. The driver had sat and waited, checking with the staff as to my situation every half hour, so he instinctively knew that this was an important meeting for me. On the drive to Shoreditch, every time the conversation would falter, Joe, the driver, would comment on a landmark as we headed through the city. We dropped Sheena and her friend outside the friend's house. Joe was so perceptive that as Sheena alighted, he said, 'Here is the pen and paper that you asked for, Mr Hardy, for the lady's telephone number.'

Sheena said thank you, took the paper and wrote down her number. She said, 'I am always home by six but try any time.' She kissed her fingers and placed them on my lips. Joe drove me home. Joe is still driving but is now on the payroll of a very grateful software house.

I cannot describe the hours I spent gazing at Sheena's phone number and how much time I wasted at the office plucking up courage to phone, but eventually, I did.

Sheena answered immediately almost before it had rung, and I do not even remember talking. Our first date was an afternoon at the Science Museum followed by an evening concert at the Albert Hall. We had an hour and a half between wandering out of the museum and the start of the concert, so we had a pizza in South Kensington, near the Tube station. Having just seen the Apollo module at the museum; we soon had the napkin covered in formulae. We were discussing how primitive the computing power of the late sixties was, compared to the mathematical power of the human brain. We were trying to work out the trajectories needed to exit near-earth orbit. Needless to say, we missed the start of the concert and just stayed chatting.

Sheena was an actuary and she changed my life but not before one other person reappeared and as usual, brought some baggage.

## Attachment 8

## BRIXMIS

**A P Stein**

My parents were both doctors in the Royal Army Medical Corps during the war and served in Egypt. They were repatriated in 1945 and I was born some months thereafter. My grandparents had all been Jewish but both my parents had denounced their faith, and indeed, all faiths. Despite this, I was baptised into the Church of England, which is why I presume I was admitted to Durham Chorister School and then as a King's Scholar at Durham School. I excelled at Greek and Latin but decried all sport. I studied at Exeter College, Oxford and took a first in mods and greats. I married Jocasta in 1973. We had met in our first term at Oxford. Jocasta read theology and was to go on to teach and write on the subject, becoming quite an expert in her chosen field. I was mildly indifferent to religion and to what she did, and whilst we were never unhappy, we were never happy. Jocasta did introduce me to Brahms, Liszt and my absolute favourite, Mendelssohn.

After graduation, I passed my Civil Service entrance exams and was "fast tracked", which meant I never stayed in any position for more than two years and so could not either make a difference or, more importantly, make any mistakes. The Civil Service likes a safe pair of hands, and I was ultra-cautious. Our summer holidays were spent sitting in a villa in Greece. Greek holidays were spent reading and visiting archaeological sites. We inherited from Jocasta's parents what could best be described as a glorified beach hut near Arklow, just south of Dublin on the coast. The Irish breaks consisted of more reading and, for me, fishing. Much of my time was spent in London, whilst Jocasta was in Oxford. We had drifted apart and it was convenient for us both to be separate. I started reading *Das Boot* in the original German and this reawakened my passion for languages that I had all but lost following university. I continued this passion of reading classics in the mother tongue and moved on to *Anna Karenina*. I had little experience of Cyrillic script, but soon found I could master written Russian and could get by when speaking.

Jocasta and I were never really close enough emotionally and physically to want or have children but our lives were changed by a tragedy. Jocasta's younger sister and her husband were travelling back to the West Country on the A30 when a driver coming in the opposite direction crossed over the centre of the road and hit them. The coroner's inquest described how the occupant of the other car "may have fallen asleep", but nothing was conclusive. The driver and both Gina and Ralf were killed. Gina and Ralf had twin daughters aged 12 at Westonhall School, Gina and Rosie, and we inherited them. I say we, but the tragedy occurred just before I was posted to West Germany. I had been at the Ministry of Defence in Whitehall. I had been given three weeks compassionate "adoption" leave and on my return was invited to join the British Commanders-in-Chief Mission to the Soviet Forces in Germany BRIXMIS. Whilst this was a military liaison mission which operated behind the Iron Curtain, it was administered by the Ministry of Defence.

BRIXMIS was meant to be no more than 31 members of staff; 11 officers, most in uniform and no more than 20 others. These staff were issued passes allowing freedom of travel and circulation, with the exception of certain restricted areas, within each other's occupation zone. So BRIXMIS would be in East Berlin and East Germany and the Soviet equivalent, SOXMIS, would operate in West Berlin and West Germany. These "tours", as they were known, were carried out in uniform and in clearly marked vehicles, not unlike police cars, but in our case marked BRIXMIS with a union flag prominently (or sometimes not so prominently) displayed.

Whilst it was never admitted by either side, any liaison of

this nature created a chance to gather information and military intelligence through reconnaissance and surveillance. There was also the occasional "requisitioning" of military material that had not been tied down. This petty opportunism was taken advantage of by both sides.

BRIXMIS was behind the Iron Curtain. It could feel the "zeitgeist" and "measure the temperature" of the Soviet Union's intentions from the front line of international espionage. However, and perhaps more importantly for me, as the civil servant in situ, it offered a conduit for communication between West and East. I had the unique role in this secondary, but crucial role of liaison. This was ironically the initial reason for the establishment of BRIXMIS, but it had been somewhat hijacked by the uniformed military.

BRIXMIS's permanent presence was supposedly in the Mission House in Potsdam, an East Germany town some 45 minutes from Berlin, depending on what part of the divided city we were heading into. The original Potsdam Mission House at Wildpark was damaged during a well-orchestrated riot against the British Forces' presence in 1958. The new building at 34 Seestrasse was given by the Soviet government, together with a sum of money as "an apology". The actual headquarters and operational centre where I was to work was in West Berlin. This was in a London Block, a part of the 1936 Olympic Stadium buildings which housed the military government of the British sector of Berlin.

So, whilst Jocasta bonded with our two new children, I headed east to what I can safely say was the first adrenaline surge of my life.

It was whilst at BRIXMIS that I met my minder Sergei Agafonov. I knew Sergei was KGB; in fact, he made no secret of it to me. He assumed I was from the British Security Services. I was always happy to admit I was a civil servant, as it was true, but denied being a "spy". But as I was to learn, you are what people want to think you are. I was dealing in "humint". Human intelligence to a certain degree, but mostly I was listening. I liked Sergei because he was razor sharp and he was always happy to introduce me to his friends and family. He was from St Petersburg and was cultured, not that the two are connected. He had no truck with his didactic Muscovite superiors and was always at pains to relate this to me. He told me that Agafonov was from the Greek meaning kindness and goodness and that one day he would return to St Petersburg and bask in Russian culture.

I was never sure how much of what Sergei said and did was to gain my confidence. He did caution me against certain bars in East Berlin but as I never went out drinking, it was of little consequence. I was always happy to provide Sergei with duty free cigarettes and King Edward cigars. I am convinced that the lure of these wooden cigar boxes achieved more for BRIXMIS in my two years than the rest of the team staff achieved since 1949 when the mission was opened. Most of our time was spent just driving about to see what was happening in the dark corners of the East German state. Our cars were Opal Senators and they were constantly tracked. We called the trips "tours" and when we were found in places where we should not be, we were usually chased and, if caught, arrested and held in detention at the nearest *Kommandatura*. The risk to persistent offenders was that they might have their passes withdrawn. This never happened on my watch and the teams were warned to, where possible, stay within acceptable boundaries of both location and behaviour. BRIXMIS was in the most part entirely overt, all personnel, all military staff wore uniform and travelled in marked cars. There were occasions when the officer and the other rank, usually a staff sergeant, would leave the driver in the vehicle and head off on foot, deliberately obscuring or hiding their identity. When our cars were chased, because they were of such superior quality and performance, they were able to shake off what was usually the East German State Security Service (Stasi). We called these the "narks" and they were as disliked by Sergei and his team as much as they were by us. The ground operations tours were conducted on an ad hoc basis or as directed by Defence Intelligence via me from London.

We did have one notable coup on my watch. Captain Russell Hill had the presence of mind to measure the calibre of the 30 mm gun of the then brand new BMP-2 armoured personnel carrier, by pressing a pear from his lunch box into it and taking an impression.

Incidents of open hostility, such as being physically attacked or shot at, or having the vehicle deliberately rammed, were rare, but they all happened at least once during my two years. All were pre-planned and were usually a distraction created to satisfy a political agenda. Unlike our Soviet counterparts, SOXMIS, we did not have any capacity to handle agents so there were never any expulsions.

Most official liaison consisted of formal events attended by both sides, for example, the Queen's birthday parade, receptions at the Mission House, and a Remembrance Day service at the Stahnsdorf War Cemetery, just east of Potsdam. There were regular wreath-laying visits to the British memorials at the former concentration camps of Ravensbrück. Buchenwald, and Sachsenhausen.

We did have informal contact through a series of parties. These were usually in celebration of some event and we would invite Sergei and his other colleagues in the Soviet External Relations Branch (SERB).

If you held a full "touring" pass, which I did, you could

go on what we called a "cultural tour", in which we and our families could stay away from the headquarters, usually for a couple of nights. We could stay in hotels in one or two cities in East Germany. I went to both Magdeburg and Leipzig. These trips offered me a great opportunity to get to know members of the Soviet and East German armed forces and civilians who I might not have otherwise met. However, once we had left Potsdam, we were on our own. We had no contact with the headquarters, so we had to deal with any unforeseen problems ourselves.

Leipzig held a fascination for me because it had links to Mendelssohn. Music had been such an important feature of the city and home of the Landeskonservatorium, the Felix Mendelssohn Bartholdy College of Music and Theatre.

I had a strange affinity with Mendelssohn as his father Abraham Mendelssohn had renounced the family's Jewish religion prior to Felix's birth and Felix was not circumcised, in defiance of the rites. It was this same strange defiance that stopped my parents having me circumcised. I must have been the first man in generations of the Stein family to have a foreskin. Mendelssohn and I had something in common.

Leipzig was subject to Arabisation by the Nazis. Beginning in 1933 and increasing in 1939, Jewish business owners were initially forced to give up their possessions and stores, but this increased in magnitude until Jews were evicted from their own homes. Many moved to Judenhäuser, which were smaller houses in the ghetto. Carl Friedrich Goerdeler, the elected mayor of Leipzig, was well known as an opponent of the Nazi regime. He resigned in 1937 when his Nazi deputy ordered the destruction of the city's statue of Felix Mendelssohn. On 20 December 1937, after the Nazis took control of the city, they renamed it Reichsmessestadt Leipzig, meaning the "Imperial Trade Fair City Leipzig". Goerdeler was executed by the Nazis in February 1945. Mendelssohn was not even a practising Jew.

My hatred of the Nazis struck a chord with Sergei and most of the Soviet members of SERB. They had a low regard for the East Germans who they felt were still complicit in the Great Patriotic war. Sergei once confessed that he had more in common with the British Officers than he did with the East Germans. He said that there was an "affinity of elites". I had to point out that that statement did not sit well with his communist credentials. I had mentioned my love of Mendelssohn to Sergei and a desire to visit Leipzig. He admitted to having a passing interest in my composer but wanted me to visit St Petersburg so I could discover the Big Five, The Mighty Five, The Russian Five, and in Russian the Moguchaya Kuchka ("The Mighty Little Heap"), a group of composers from St Petersburg who came together in the 1860s to create what they wanted to call the authentic national sound. The new nationalistic music was to distinguish itself from the so called western music typified by German lieder and Italian opera. I knew of Modest Mussorgsky, Nikolai Rimsky-Korsakov and Alexander Borodin, but had not heard of the other two Mily Balakirev and César Cui. Sergei promised to widen my musical education.

The German Democratic Republic had a centrally planned economy, but Leipzig was not part of any structured plan. Before the Second World War, Leipzig had developed a balanced and varied type of industry and businesses and services thrived. Sadly, during the period of the German Democratic Republic, the heavy hand of the state concentrated all the dirty heavy industry there and so it was smoggy and smelly. Leipzig was not an attractive city to live in, nor to visit.

My visit was initiated by a message from London. There were "prayers for peace" at St Nicholas Church in Leipzig, established as part of the peace movement in East Germany. London simply asked me to attend and see what was happening. No more, no less. I was given no names, no guidance. I was just to go to "see what is happening".

At this time, trade fairs were held at a site in the south of the city, near the Monument to the Battle of the Nations. I thought a trip to a trade fair was more plausible with a visit to a church as an additional attraction, rather than a visit to church with a trade fair as an additional attraction. With either plan I could also visit the monument which was erected to commemorate the Battle of Leipzig. My colleague, a young captain in the Intelligence Corps, gave me a suggested brief based on a long weekend he had spent in Leipzig and it included hotels and places of interest. He said that his idea of a weekend break and my idea were probably some distance apart and that I should not follow the brief too closely. I had once been erroneously shown the report that this captain had sent to his commanding officer several weeks after my arrival. It had a paragraph which described me as "if Carlsberg did boring, it would be Stein". This was, I was told, a reference to a television advert but I understood the sentiment.

Truth be known, I was boring but was quite happy in my own company. I was not seeking thrills or adventure. I was doing my job and I had satisfaction in a job well done. I was excited about heading off on my own. A solo trip did breach guidelines, but no-one would have wanted to go with me except Jocasta and then it would have been the church that was the attraction. She was now totally absorbed in the lives of the twins.

It was the Leipzig trip which was to change my life. I discovered vodka. I now add orange but back then it was cold, neat and it almost killed me.

## Attachment 9

## Problems

*If you were an 18th century Caribbean pirate ship captain, your modus operandi would be to monitor an incoming vessel's nationality and then raise a similar flag so the vessel was fooled. As the vessel came within striking distance, you would raise the pirate colours and mount an attack on the unsuspecting target. You would send your pirates onto the vessel, fighting first on deck and then going below to force a surrender. For the brave pirate, the action of leaving the bright sunlit deck and heading below would be night blindness. Until the eyes were accustomed to the dark, the pirate was blind. The problem was remedied by wearing a patch over one eye. Once the fighting above deck was over, the pirate went below, lifted the eye patch and could fight on equal terms as the crew below. So that is the explanation for the eye patch; but why the parrot? That is another story – written by Robert Louis Stevenson.*

**Ryan Haston**

I was not good at following orders, but I upped and left my flat. Lela was not happy but to show I was not leaving her in the lurch, I left my expensive Brompton folding bike and most of my clothes. I told her I would be back to settle up soon and would need the room in the future.

Lela was not really with it. She did not do mornings. I did not really know what she did. She did not own the house but was given reduced rent for administering it. I had started to grow a beard as I had failed to buy any razor blades so I looked pretty scruffy when I turned up at my "alternative accommodation" near Madam YoJo's. I hadn't planned on staying long and had everything I needed stuffed into an old army kitbag. I was shown a room with a couple of beds; one had a man sleeping in it, so I presumed the other was mine.

That evening, I reported to the Bohemian and asked for the manager. The Bohemian was brighter and cleaner than I expected but it could have done with a coat of paint. The doorman was polite and friendly, as was the manager to whom I reported. Steve, the manager, did not ask any questions, which was just as well, as I had no answers to any that might have been posed. Quentin, the artistic director, was more concerned. He had full artistic control over the burlesque show and had wanted to audition everyone himself. He was at pains to point out that his grievance was not with me, but the "powers that be". The fact that I seemed to be an established "Shakespearean actor" proved just enough to satisfy him. He did state that I "might do". He asked if I was growing a beard or was just scruffy. I assured him I would shave before any performance, unless he wanted me to play King Lear.

Quentin proceeded to liken my role in the show to Chorus, the single character dressed in black in Shakespearean plays to help the audience follow the action. To try and gauge him, I grunted, 'Do you bite your thumb at me, sir?'

'No, sir,' replied Quentin, 'but I bite my thumb.'

We both grinned. I was on the team, even if it was as the Master of Ceremonies in a bawdy romp with much dancing (with half a chorus line), a girl who could hoola-hoop with 30 or more hoops and a siren who sang haunting ballads. Both the chanteuse and the hoola-hoop girl were scantily clad and I did think that hoola-hooping looked rather painful. Other acts were woven into the show and some were removed as and when necessary. It all seemed rather random but Quentin seemed to know what he was doing and there were always enough punters buying drinks and watching to make evenings interesting.

Spotting Mr Stein was not difficult. He was a regular on a Friday night and dressed exactly as I thought a civil servant should dress on a night out in the West End. White T-shirt and black leather bomber jacket. I was in no hurry to meet my target. In fact, I wanted Stein to meet me and maybe make the first overture rather than vice versa. It would be too obvious if I moved first. I thought I should act counter-intuitively and suppress my usual bonhomie but I had forgotten how poor my acting was. I was enjoying the new work. I started nervously on the first night but as the week wore on, I relaxed and improved. This was not my self-assessment but that of the manager and Quentin.

My first introduction to Stein was during a show some three weeks after I had started. The burlesque siren was crooning *Maybe this time* from *Cabaret* and slinking about the audience. She dripped herself and her feather boa around Stein's neck. Stein seemed to enjoy the attention, contrary to the attributes that Robert had suggested. When the act was over, I arranged a drink to be sent over to Stein for having been such a good sport. Stein was not a big drinker, according to the barman, but would be happy with a screwdriver, a mixture of vodka and orange. When the drink was given to Stein, I raised a glass to him from the edge of the stage. It had been my habit to close the show by introducing one act as the encore. As the burlesque siren was doing the curtain call, I asked her if she would not mind reintroducing herself. She was delighted and it gave me the chance to go into the audience. At the end of the number, I positioned myself so I could move towards Stein. As the applause died down, I moved. I gave a brief introduction and then asked Stein for some feedback on the show. I explained that as a regular customer, his views were important. Stein was reticent and did not have very much to say about the show itself but was quite animated about some of the acts he had enjoyed over the several months he had been attending. I was careful to be short and brief as I wanted everything to seem natural. I made a point of questioning several people that night. All were near Stein.

I was rather pleased with myself at the time, but I realised how even the simplest thing can be picked up to catch you out. Stein was to tell me some months later that he knew I had singled him out that night. I had been perplexed until Stein reminded me that he had been the only member of the audience to be rewarded with a drink. He had had a screwdriver sent over, which was his favourite drink. I mentally noted that I was only ever going to be a poor actor and an even poorer agent. I also realised Stein was no fool.

The truth is Stein was an easy target for me thereafter, as he seemed to like my company. Stein took to staying for a drink after the show and I would join him "when able". I did not want to be too intrusive too early. Stein was happy to be called AP and was happy to chat about his wife and children in Frome. He was less happy talking about his job, save that he admitted working for the government. He seemed to prefer male company and was rather uncomfortable when any of the chorus line or female artistes joined us for a drink. I once challenged AP as to the attraction of burlesque and he gave me a curious reply: 'I want my obituary in *The Times* to be interesting; remember Elsie was the happiest corpse Sally Bowles had ever seen!'

## Attachment 10

## Appearances

*For a little mischief, Charlie Chaplin entered a "Charlie Chaplin look-a-like" contest in Switzerland: little did he expect to come third. Perhaps it is understandable, as the winner probably exaggerated Chaplin's mannerisms and therefore seemed more authentic to the judges. We still live in a society where we are immediately categorised by what we wear, how we speak and how we dress. What is surprising is how few people realise that without changing very much, they can significantly change how other people view them. Archibald Leach was a humble boy from Bristol, but through the medium of film he was turned into the suave, relaxed, American sophisticated Cary Grant. He once confided that 'everyone wants to be Cary Grant, even I want to be Cary Grant.'*

*Mick Jagger cultivated the image of a wild rock star with everything carried out to excess. His prowess as a lover seemed legendary until punctured by a female groupie who reported back, 'He was great, but he was no Mick Jagger.'*

### Gordon Shawcross

I thought I had recovered from my stranger than fiction treason Saturday, but I kept getting flashbacks. I had periods of anxiety and often felt more upset during them than I did during the confrontation. There was no one I could discuss it with at the office and the more I thought about it, the more stupid it seemed. I even started to doubt that it had happened and wondered if it was some false memory syndrome. I had no idea if such a syndrome existed but whatever had happened was not normal. No one in Britain gets picked up off the street and accused of treason and then is released as if nothing had happened. I had heard nothing from Haston and despite my brief moment of clarity when I had headed to the West End, I was at a loss to know what to do next or more importantly whether I should do anything else. I had three facts; Lela's telephone number, the note from Haston and Hardy's address. I felt I had nothing to lose by following up the latter. I would look up my old friend Geordie.

According to the Old Boys' secretary, Mr Hardy had moved from Albert Mansions to Harcourt Terrace, which was London SW5. I looked at my A to Z and discovered it was in Earl's Court or that seemed to be the nearest Tube. The following Saturday morning, I set off to find Hardy. I assumed that Hardy would have been living in shared accommodation, probably with a couple of Australians and working for a radical newspaper. I had no idea why I had pre-judged Hardy and was curious to find out how right I was. I had written a note to shove through his letter box if he was not in.

Harcourt Terrace is near the Boltons; it is not in Earl's Court but almost in Chelsea. The designated house was beautiful. It did not seem to have been turned into flats. I knew it was seriously expensive. I checked my A to Z at least three times before knocking, as I was sure this could not be Hardy's address. A girl answered and said, 'Yes?'

I apologised for the unannounced call but explained that I was seeking an old school friend, Geordie Hardy, and maybe I had the wrong house.

The girl said, 'No, you have the right house, but Pete has gone to buy a newspaper. Please come in.' I was ushered into a beautiful Georgian drawing room with a bay window and a most unusual lamp shade.

'Would you like a cup of tea or coffee? I am Sheena, by the way, Pete's fiancée.' Sheena had a "Morningside Accent" which was the posh side of Edinburgh.

I said, 'I love this house,' having no idea whose house it was. Sheena just smiled. 'I also love that lampshade,' I added.

At this, Sheena laughed and said, 'It is a rhombicosidodecahedron; it is the reason Pete and I met.' She worked out from my vacant response that the shape was lost on me.

I was happy to offer, 'Well, Geordie was the mathematician, that's for sure. He could recite Pi to 120 decimal points and won a school prize for that.'

'Did he?' Sheena responded, adding, 'Well, he kept that quiet. What other gems can I find out about my intended before he gets back?'

One wall was covered in books and the librarian in me started to browse as Sheena made the coffee. They were nearly all on mathematics and computing. There was not one classic novel, nor one work of fiction. It was a library straight from NASA. I was so absorbed by the complex titles that I did not notice Geordie walk into the room.

'So to what de we owe this intrusion, bonny lad?' Geordie put on his strongest accent and shook my hand. He then uncharacteristically gripped me in a hug and I found myself reciprocating.

'Gentlemen, you are pleased to see each other,' joked a smiling Sheena, as she returned with a tray. 'I have added some Jammie Dodgers that I was saving for the Brownies to remind you two of school days,' she added.

Strangely, the conversation started with Geoff Farnthwait. Geordie had cut his obituary from the *Evening Gazette* that his Dad had sent down to him. We were both surprised that this towering icon of our youth had never been to university but had gone to a teacher training college after National Service. He had been one of seven sons born to a pitman from near Doncaster and had lost four elder brothers in the forces during the Second World War. We discussed how far removed our impression and memory of Farnthwait was from the obituary. It was at this point that Geordie said, 'And mind you, who would have thought I would be living in the swankiest part of London with a beautiful lass?'

'The house is beautiful… and so is Sheena,' I added, quickly realising how ungallant the statement sounded. Luckily, they both laughed.

'So Gordon, what are you up to? Can you stay for tea?' I knew that Geordie meant dinner and was about to say yes, when Sheena cut in, saying, 'He means dinner.'

I grinned. 'I know, I am a northern boy, too.'

Sheena added, 'But you are polished!' I stayed for tea/dinner. Geordie and Sheena were the two most engaging people I had ever met. They had a preposterous disagreement over analemmatic sundials, a subject where I could only spectate. I found that I could laugh with them and they were happy that I laughed at them. They had such an esoteric passion for themselves and gnomons. Having had far too much Newcastle Brown Ale, I ended up staying in the spare room. The room, if it had not been spinning, and I could have measured it, would have been larger than the whole of my flat.

Haston had come up in conversation, mainly as a backstory to how Sheena and Geordie met. They met at Mark's wedding and this led on back to Mark's party and the story of the orange. I was reminded by Geordie of what a hero I had been and found myself blushing, even after so many years. Sheena and Geordie were such good company and entertained me so well that I kept putting off discussing my recent run-in with Haston.

Geordie was back out getting the Sunday newspapers when me and my throbbing head came down to breakfast. Sheena told me that I was getting a full Scottish, whether I liked it or not! Sheena was pleased that I had stayed, as she had learnt more about Pete in one night from me than she had learnt in twelve months from Pete.

It was over breakfast that Sheena really caught my attention. She said to me, 'I have got it. I have been racking my brains to remember who I spoke to at Mark's wedding about you. It was Mark's sister Caroline.' Sheena laughed as she told me that had Caroline had her way, she may have been married to Mark's accountant. Sheena recalled how Caroline had pointed out the accountant who was down on a table next to Geordie. Caroline thought that an actuary like Sheena and an accountant would be well suited. Caroline had noticed Geordie sitting on the same table and related the orange incident. Sheena told me that Geordie sounded far more interesting and wanted to meet one of that crowd. Caroline told Sheena that she had first met Geordie at the party and how the orange incident had ruined her evening, not least because she had met a wonderful man. The wonderful man was subsequently evicted from the party with Geordie even after he had saved a man's life.

I blushed again and used the mention of the incident to explain that Haston was the reason why I wanted to meet up with Geordie. I wanted to explain what had happened to me the week before. Both Sheena and Geordie listened as I recalled the meeting on the Friday night and the Saturday adventure. What I described started to sound more and more like a fairy story. Even when I finished, they said nothing. Geordie broke the silence by asking if I still had Haston's note. I took it out of my wallet. Geordie confessed that the story sounded so implausible that he wanted to see Haston's note to make sure it was not the Brown Ale still talking.

They both studied the note and Sheena read it out:

*Dear Shawcross,*

*Thank you for saving my skin. As usual, much ado about nothing, I have been as "civil as an orange". I will explain.*

*Jaffa*

I did tell them that I felt such a fool, especially standing in the church fête watching the Pimlico house. Sheena wanted to know what I wanted Pete to do. I confessed that my main worry was whether Haston was in trouble, but that I was also curious as to what mess Haston had got himself into. I also confessed that I had had many an allegation thrown at me over the years but I had never been accused of treason.

## Attachment 11

## Gathering

**Peter (Geordie) Hardy**

Treason did seem a little dramatic. I had harboured socialist thoughts that included the overthrow of the government, but treason made me think of the gunpowder plot. I leaned back on my regency dining room carver until I was brought back to earth by a reprimand from Sheena. I was listening to a friend that I had not seen for over a decade spouting this far-fetched tale round my table. I was still a man of very few words but given his strange encounter with Haston, I felt an urge to relate to Gordon my reunion with Haston. It too had been bizarre, but not as bizarre as Gordon's.

My accountant was concerned that my company was making too much money and paying too much tax. He suggested some tax mitigation strategies. The accountant had advised donating to charity and/or establishing a trust. My accountant had wanted me to consider offshore investments but there was too much socialism left in me to countenance that.

The suggestion of a donation to charity had other effects on me. It shone a light into how shallow my life was and if it was not for Sheena, heaven knows what I would be like. I had never given to charity before and could not even think of a charity to donate to. With Sheena's help, I decided to focus on charities that could help children like me or should I say like me when I was a young Geordie. We started to think about organisations that we felt might make a difference. I loved my time as a DJ and loved music but this had not been developed at school – it had started at the orange party. I decided that my old school was too obsessed with Latin and Greek and it needed a music, art and drama facility. The school, which was no longer the grammar school of my youth, was now a comprehensive but in some way, this strengthened my resolve. The upshot was that under legal and accounting guidance, I was to establish the Edward Hardy Trust, named after Thumper. The trust would build a creative art building on the northern side of the school quadrangle. My accountant was pleased, as it meant that with the tax relief, much of the financial burden was carried by the treasury. Of course, the school were delighted and both Sheena and I had been invited to meet with the headteacher and the chair of governors for a lunch, as they were keen to show their gratitude. On Sheena's suggestion, I invited the school to appoint two trustees to the board. They were thrilled to do so and nominated one of the deputy heads; there were now three. The school also asked if one trustee could be an "Old Boy" and offered one who was involved in the arts. The Old Boy was a member of the Royal Shakespeare Company and the school were very proud of his achievements. His name was Sean Cross. I asked which year he had been in and the school said they would provide me with a profile, but they never did.

Sean Cross's deed of appointment to the trust was

drawn up by Mark's law firm and they did the appropriate due diligence. They, the lawyers, noted that Sean Cross was a stage name and the actual name was Ryan Haston. The lawyers never told me this. The first trustee meeting was held in London at Mark's law firm and both Sheena and I went. We had lunch with Mark beforehand, as the meeting was scheduled for 2 o'clock. The law firm was off Cheapside and as lunch took longer than anticipated, Mark, Sheena and I had to run back to the office. Mark kept telling me that I was the client and it was my meeting so we could be as late as I liked, but I was obsessed with punctuality and was adamant that we were back for 2 o'clock.

As we piled into the lift, we were joined by a tall, handsome besuited chap with a black calf leather briefcase and a younger man with a pile of loose-leaf files. The younger man exited on the first floor. I looked at the tall man and thought he looked like the archetypal London lawyer from his shiny black brogues to his blond hair and blue eyes. His shoes were handmade, and I wondered if they were from the same shop in Jermyn Street where I had had mine made. I smiled as I looked down at my shoes and wondered if he had noticed mine. As I looked into the blue eyes, I felt a wave of panic. I felt dirty, I felt one of the great unwashed. It was Sheena who felt me shrinking towards her as the lift doors opened. Sheena instinctively found she had her protective arm around me.

We all walked to the Denning Conference Room on the third floor and the tall man came in behind us. Mark introduced himself to the stranger who replied, 'Sean Cross, but for the benefit of the meeting, I think I am Ryan Haston.'

I regained my composure. I looked at my Rolex on my wrist. It had replaced the Timex as my comfort blanket. I remembered that this was my meeting and I was funding the trust. Mark introduced me and Haston was delighted to be reacquainted. He rushed round the side of the desk and shook my hand and was unbelievably "hail fellow well met".

'So you have been dragooned into being a trustee, too,' he enthused. Haston continued to say how he was looking forward to meeting Edward Hardy as it was such a kind gesture to help the old school. I was happy to let Haston sound off, especially as he was genuinely pleased to see me; either that or he was an excellent actor. I offered this as a quip when I got a word in and Haston laughed. 'Trust me, I am a dreadful actor. I have just returned from a tour of Eastern Europe and I only ever carried a spear.'

Sheena asked about the Royal Shakespeare Company.

Haston roared, 'Heavens no, it was a touring Shakespeare company' and 'I am now resting.'

Mark also reminded Haston that he and Haston had met. He mentioned their fathers had been Masonic Lodge members together and Haston had been to Mark's parents' house. At that point, Haston put his head in his hands. It was the first time Haston had been anything but dynamic. Mark needed to say no more, and in any event, a receptionist was now showing my accountant and three more members to the meeting. I quite took to Haston and so did Sheena and the meeting went well. Mark was such a good chairman of the meeting that whilst he talked of the donor, he never disclosed that it was my company and more specifically me, that were putting up the money. If Haston linked the surname Hardy to mine, he never showed it.

I described the meeting to Gordon and particularly my initial nausea on seeing Haston. I never discussed emotions, even to Sheena, and was pleased that for the first time I was talking about my feelings without being self-conscious. I felt quite proud of myself and all the more so because Sheena kept squeezing my hand as I spoke. I had skated over the finer points of the trust, but Gordon was no fool and I am sure he was able to fill in all the gaps.

It was Sheena that was able to complete the reunion picture. Some months after the trust was established, Haston had phoned our house in a panic. Sheena answered because I was up in Middlesbrough. I was organising a new retirement bungalow for Thumper because he had mobility issues and couldn't climb his stairs. Sheena offered to help Haston. Seemingly, he was starting a new job and needed a trusted address in central London. His current digs were shared with other actors and his mail was going missing. He just needed a couple of weeks until he had arranged his new house. Sheena said it seemed a reasonable request and so she was about to agree to this house but then offered an alternative. I had kept hold of my flat in Albert Mansions as I thought it a good investment now the London property prices were rocketing. I had not arranged a tenant at that point, so Sheena suggested Haston used that address. Joe, one of my staff, checked the flat every week and he could pick up any mail. I have to say I was less than pleased with Sheena when she told me.

I reminded Sheena that we did not know Haston and Haston could have had countless other places to pick up post, ranging from the Post Office to his work. Despite my misgivings over the assistance to Haston, I was pleased that Sheena was so kind and helpful and it reminded me just how lucky I was. I leant over to give Sheena a kiss as I said this, but she just threw a napkin at me and laughed.

Gordon had sat and listened to my recollection in silence. I do not think I had ever been in company and spoken for so long, especially relating a story. Gordon asked about Mark. Sheena and I were happy to update him. Gordon seemed to blush when Sheena mentioned Caroline, Mark's sister. Sheena picked up on this too and probed further.

Seemingly, Gordon thought of Caroline as his "first love". She was the first girl he had ever spoken to and who had enjoyed his company. Caroline had had an impact on him as it was clear that Gordon was embarrassed by his revelation. I think Sheena realised Gordon's discomfort and so nothing further was mentioned. Sheena told me some time later that Gordon had been desperate to ask more questions about her but felt too self-conscious. As the weekend gathering came to a close, we had one last discussion about Haston. We agreed that, if only to satisfy Gordon's curiosity, we would try and find out what happened to Haston and why Gordon was almost hung for treason.

I said I would arrange for Joe to collect the post from Albert Mansions on the Monday, and we would gather again in a week's time. Sheena thought this was too long if Haston was in trouble and suggested we all three met on the Tuesday night. Sheena and I were going to Ceroc that night anyway at Wandsworth Town Hall which was just round the corner from the flat. Gordon could join us as he was only in Streatham. I had to explain to Gordon that Ceroc was a dance craze that Sheena and I had been introduced to by Mark's wife Francesca. A crowd now went on a Tuesday evening to do "rock and roll" style dancing introduced from France. Sheena insisted that Gordon join us for Ceroc, despite his protestations. We would go after we had been to pick up the post from the flat. I had not seen the flat for a while and wanted to check everything was in good order before I started to rent it out.

## Attachment 12

## Dancing

**Gordon Shawcross**

I had known Geordie for just over five years at school; I had just spent two days with him and had heard him speak more in two days than that whole five years. I knew he had a Geordie accent and he had always helped me with my maths (and physics and chemistry, if the truth be known), but I had never really heard him speak and certainly he had never told me a story. I liked him and I liked Sheena and if I was going to solve this mystery, I could not think of two better people to assist me. I felt somewhat sad that there were actually very few people that I knew that I could have asked to help. I had my flatmate and I knew he could not help unless he had a written authority to do so from his girlfriend. I had a couple of friends at work, but they were limited to the occasional retreat to the pub as they commuted from Essex and Crawley. I had friends at the squash club, but everything revolved around squash and the squash socials. In fact, this incident had highlighted to me just how narrow my friendship group had become. The incident – I had not settled on what to call it – had come at just the right time and I was suddenly looking forward to the adventure. Geordie and Sheena had believed me. I was not going mad. I felt invigorated.

Tuesday evening had never figured in my social life. It

was probably the most depressing night of the week. It didn't even have the hollow grin of Wednesday as being past halfway through the week. I had a niggle that I hardly knew Geordie socially. Sheena was even more of a new acquaintance. I was concerned that I would go to the Ceroc, be a wallflower when not dancing and an embarrassment when dancing. This did not bode well.

I could not believe how quickly Tuesday arrived. I had left work slightly late, delayed by a phone call that I could not shake off. I had no idea what one wore to do French "rock and roll". I laid out a pair of stone-coloured trousers and a new shirt that was still in the package and had a shower. I thought I was fully dried from the shower but the new shirt stuck to my back as I pulled it on. It was obvious that it was a new shirt as the creases were distinct across the front, so I took it off and ironed it. This also dried the back and made it warm when I put it back on. There were no convenient Tubes for me to get to Geordie's flat and then onto Ceroc, so I decided to go by pushbike. The front tyre was flat but once I had pumped it up, it seemed good to go. I put an elastic band around my right ankle to keep my trousers off the chain. It did look overcast but I did not want a bulky coat with me so grabbed a tweed jacket. I guessed it was a 20-minute ride but I was disorientated near Tooting Bec and I ended up almost an hour in the saddle. Meeting Geordie and Sheena was no problem, as they were already at the flat when I arrived. I could see that Geordie was irritated by my tardiness and I had to apologise a couple of times. He did let me take my bike up the stairs to the first floor, so it was safe. It was a beautiful two bedroomed flat. For all Geordie's troubled childhood, he had certainly learnt to live well when he arrived in London.

There were three unopened letters; two addressed to Sean Cross and one to Mr R V Haston. We agreed that one seemed to be a circular and then debated whether to open the other two. The postmarks were from two days earlier, so they had not been in the flat long. Whilst I felt that this was my venture, I did think that Geordie was custodian of the letters; by agreeing they could be sent to his property. I told him that he had the last word on when they should be opened. Geordie thought that it was better not to open them yet, at least not until we had made further enquiries. Geordie suggested that we would open them at the weekend or sooner if there was not any contact from Haston. In the end, because we were running late, we just grabbed the letters and headed off to Ceroc without further discussion. Geordie and Sheena jumped in their car and I took my bike. The front tyre had lost some air so I gave it another quick pump to make sure I would reach the destination. I set off towards Wandsworth Bridge. It was April and right on cue, a torrential rain shower started, and it was not to stop until I found a wrought iron fence to fasten my bike onto outside Wandsworth Town Hall.

## Attachment 13

## Behaviour

*A wonder of the natural world is the mass migrations of animals. Two of the largest on the planet are the wildebeest of Africa and the caribou of Northern America. The common theme to both mass migrations is that they are started by the tiniest of mosquitoes. The herds move to avoid the irritation caused by creatures they can hardly see. When an attractive woman showed too much interest in Zeus, Zeus's wife Hera knew how to see her off – she set a gadfly against her.*

**A P Stein**

No matter how much I had tried to vary the programme, I was restricted by the opening times of the trade fair, the evening meeting in St Nicholas Church and the access to the monument. It meant following the suggested itinerary that Hill had given to me, I would have one less evening in Leipzig and only a passing visit to the monument. I did not really mind as at least I was doing something different. The car park at the trade fair was huge but almost empty. I knew that it was not going to be vibrant, but I had hoped to be entertained or educated. It was easy to wander round as there were no crowds and no queues. The trade fair was lifeless. The East Germans had little to sell, except to the internal market. This was an international trade fair but East Germany had nothing that anyone wanted to buy, save for some camera lenses.

A new brown Trabant car was the focal point and this seemed to me to be made from compressed cardboard. Everything was so dull. It was a monochrome "exhibition" that was a decade older than any West German equivalent. My German was good enough for me to pose technical questions to the Trabant salesman but that meant it was good enough to arouse suspicion and so I was only ever going to receive basic answers. I started to feel rather depressed. If this was the best that East Germany had to offer as a vision for the future, surely the populace would revolt. Increasingly, East Germans were watching West German television. Surely, they could not be happy living under a colourless, oppressive regime. I took one last look at the Trabant and thought, no the country is not colourless; the country is brown and brown is an appropriate colour for this shitty country. I walked back to my car just as it started to rain.

The Monument to the Battle of the Nations or *Völkerschlachtdenkmal* was built to commemorate the 1813 Battle of Leipzig, also known as the Battle of the Nations. It cost six million marks and the money was raised by public subscription, rather like Nelson's

Column. It was built in 1913 for the 100th anniversary of the battle. It was particularly poignant to a divided Germany, as famously, Germans fought on both sides during the battle. Napoleon's army also included conscripted Germans. In 1813, the left bank of the Rhine had been annexed by Napoleon and these troops were considered by Napoleon to be French.

The monument commemorates Napoleon's defeat at Leipzig. This was considered by many historians to be the first sign that Napoleon was not invincible. His vulnerability would be exposed at Waterloo some two years later. It did end hostilities in what was named the War of the Sixth Coalition. The coalition of Russia, Prussia, Austria and Sweden commanded by Tsar Alexander I of Russia and Prince Karl Philipp of Schwarzenberg. The monument is said to be at the position of some of the bloodiest fighting and where Napoleon ordered his Army's retreat.

The structure is huge at almost 100 metres tall. There are steps that head up to a viewing platform, which is at the top. From the platform, there are panoramic views across Leipzig and the rolling fields and around. The monument is largely concrete covered in dark granite. It is an example of Wilhelmine architecture.

It was also the scene of some of the last fighting in

World War II, when Nazi forces in Leipzig made their last stand against US troops.

I cheered up when I arrived at the monument, as the rain had stopped. It was impressive and the 500 steps got my heart racing. It was surprisingly quiet and I would have liked to dwell on the viewing platform, but I cut it short when the weather changed. Mist reduced the visibility and I didn't feel I had the correct overcoat if it started to rain again. I drove into Leipzig and given the time, decided to park in the centre and go straight to the church as it was the reason for my trip.

The building of St Nicholas Church began in 1165. It is named after St Nicholas, patron saint of travellers and merchants. Originally, it was constructed in the Romanesque style with twin towers and was extended and enlarged in the early 16th century in the style of the time, which was Gothic. The main tower was added in 1730 and this was Baroque; the entrance dates from 1759. I gleaned the information by reading the plaque, which, although written in German, had an English translation underneath. I was particularly impressed with the entrance, as it was finished in the same year as the Battle of Minden, the turning point of the Seven Years' War.

On a separate pillar was a note that the philosopher and mathematician Gottfried Wilhelm Leibniz was "baptised here on 3 July 1646". My brain was telling me that this was when the Cavaliers and Roundheads were fighting each other during the English Civil War. I was mindful that all my knowledge was Anglo-centric. I related everything back to what was happening in Britain at these times. I was also amazed that this magnificent church was here in the middle of what is ostensibly a country without religion. The communists tolerated the church and this beautiful building stood in defiance of their beliefs.

Whilst I was mindful of the change in my family's religion, I also mused that this church had changed sides several times too. It was now Protestant, having been Roman Catholic but it allowed Catholic services to be held.

Of greatest historical interest to me was that St Nicholas was the venue for the premiere and four of the five performances of the *St John Passion* by Bach. It was also the venue for many of his cantatas and oratorios. This was one good reason to visit.

The prayer meeting was very well attended, and it was clear that the demography was half the age of a normal congregation. There was almost an evangelical verve, but it was more about the world than God. I could see why London wanted me to see what was happening. There was no rebellion or insurrection being stoked, but an individualism and call to arms. There was a vibrancy and thrill that was in stark contrast to the trade fair. I sat discretely at the back and despite missing some of the verbs at the end of sentences because the congregation clapped, I understood most of the main address. At the end, I lingered to watch people leave and I was joined by two young women.

'Ich nehme an, sie überprüfen uns – fühlen sie sich nicht schlecht?' growled one. 'Im Gegenteil, ich habe den Abend genossen,' I responded.

She had asked me if I was checking up on them and feeling bad about it.

I responded, 'On the contrary, I had enjoyed the evening.'

Whilst my German was good, my accent was not and so they both asked almost at the same time if I was American and then smiled when I replied, 'Englander!' They both visibly relaxed. They had presumed I was Stasi, and, in my overcoat, it was probably an easy mistake to make.

I had booked into a small gasthaus off Ritterstrasse as recommended by Hill and I presume it wasn't far from the church and I told my two new companions. They asked where I was going after church and I told them that a friend had recommended the Kabarett Baufunzel but that I probably would not go as my interest was more Mendelssohn. The frauleins were animated by my response and insisted that I should go to the kabarett and they would join me. They were at pains to tell me it was not like Berlin. Inge, who seemed to have the best English accent, conspiratorially confided in me that she had loved *I am a camera* by Isherwood and yes, the Baufunzel was absolutely nothing like Berlin. I never really agreed to go but then I did not stop Inge and Irme dragging me together with two other friends Thorsten and Klaus off to Nikolaistrasse.

I would never be sure what happened that night. I was taught to party by a suppressed group of people that seemed determined that I would think well of them. They all spoke remarkable English and they all had an unbelievable ability to hold their drink. The cabaret was loud and got louder and the audience that sat at tables of four got closer and closer as more tables were moved to accommodate ever-growing groups. When Thorsten heard that my surname was Stein, the glass that he had been drinking from was replaced by "Herr Ober" with an earthenware Humpen. A Humpen was a large stein that held one litre. It also had a hinged pewter lid opened by a thumb lever. I never noticed when the pilsner lager turned to schnapps and then to vodka. I enjoyed the vodka and wondered why I had not discovered it before. I did not notice when the cabaret ended. I did not notice the van that took me home. I did not remember who was with me and I had no idea where I was taken.

I woke up in a flat in a block off what I now know to be Hohne Strasse. I could not lift my head and I could not hear anything but I did think that there was no fool like an old fool. London would not be happy with any explanation. This was the classic "honeytrap", so beloved of spy novels. I was naked, apart from one black sock. I shuddered and propped myself up on one elbow. There were three or maybe four other bodies in various states of undress lying under sleeping bags and blankets around the room. I seemed to be lying on the only sofa and my trousers were draped over the back. I reached out and despite my throbbing head, managed to put them on. I couldn't find any underwear and I was desperate for the loo. I orientated myself and guessed it would be off the corridor leading to the front door. I stood up and stumbled over a body which seemed to be Inge, just below my feet at the end of the sofa. The bathroom was the first door I tried. Klaus was asleep in the bath covered with a shower curtain and a bath mat. I found myself laughing as I relieved myself. I thought, *What an idiot I am, but better to be hung for a sheep as a lamb.* I laughed out loud for thinking of this proverb, given what I was holding. I then remembered the proverb is *hanged* not *hung*. I shook my delicate head. *Why was I even thinking proverbs when I was in a compromising position that would probably cost me my career, wife, reputation and everything else I had ever stood for?*

Of all the "house guests", Irme was the most cheerful and animated. She came in from the kitchen with a coffee, which she gave to me as I sat back down of the sofa. She had a light cotton nightdress which was almost see-through and I had to avert my gaze.

'You were such fun last night, Affe, we did so enjoy your company.'

I asked where I was, what had happened and why I was Affe.

Irme was happy to explain, 'You introduce yourself as AP and all our friends thought you were Ape and Ape is Affe in German. You are at Thorsten's flat. He lives here with Inge and me.' She continued, 'You are here because you couldn't remember which gasthaus on Ritterstrasse you were staying at.'

I smiled and thanked her for the explanation and the coffee. My shirt was half down the back of the sofa and I tugged it out and put it on. It was creased badly and with my unshaven stubble I felt very embarrassed and vulnerable. I must have looked a sight. I wondered what Jocasta would have made of the situation. Irme sat next to me and asked if I wanted a slice of toast. She said that there was no food in the house apart from bread, potatoes and carrots. Klaus sat up in the corner and lit a cigarette. He offered one to Irme and me. We both declined.

Inge at my feet said that she wanted one and Klaus threw it over. I caught it and Inge clapped. I was keen to leave, so I could try and find my car. I found myself inviting them all to my gasthaus for breakfast. Inge was happy to accept, but all of the others declined. The absence of taxis meant that we had to walk back to central Leipzig, arriving in time for lunch. Inge was interesting and open. She was happy to chat about life under Honecker, the intrusive state, her yearning for freedom. I had a nagging doubt that the whole evening had been staged and that there would be revealing photos of me with Inge or even Thorsten. The more we walked and talked, the less concerned I was.

I collected my case from the car, which was still parked in the side street where I had left it. I was not sure I was fit to drive that soon after the night of alcohol. At the gasthaus, I ordered lunch for two and collected my room key from the young receptionist. Inge and I then went upstairs so I could shave and change my clothing. I needed some underwear; I was chafed after the long walk going commando. Inge sat on the bed and our conversation continued. I was telling Inge about Durham and Oxford. There was a knock on the door of the room and I answered, expecting the two plates of sandwiches I had ordered. Two policemen were standing there. They were not interested in me, but arrested Inge for breach of sub-section 249 of the criminal code for "endangering public order by anti-social behaviour". Inge looked back at me and lifted her eyebrows as she was led away. It was the last gesture she made and it was a haunting sight. I repacked and went down to the reception to check out and see what had happened to Inge. I was greeted by a short, fat gasthaus owner, who told me off, saying that prostitution was banned and forbidden in his hotel. He told me that if I wanted that type of thing, I should go to the trade fair like all the other foreigners. I remonstrated and explained I had not even stayed in the hotel and demanded to speak to the police. I was given a telephone number and a scowl.

I was troubled, deeply troubled. Should I make a scene down at the police station and turn a little local difficulty into an international incident, or should I pack up and head back to Potsdam? It was a binary decision: yes or no.

I owed Inge no loyalty, but my sense of duty had been branded onto me at school. I then started to wonder whether it was all a setup. Maybe they did take photographs, maybe they are waiting for me to storm down to the police station to try and exercise my British sense of fair play and justice.

I took the easy option and returned directly to Potsdam, but my conscience was still in Leipzig. I knew Inge's name and address; I thought I could write and offer to settle any fine she received. This assuaged my guilt somewhat. I had not slept with her. She was too young and I was not really bothered by women, not that I was bothered by men either. I often felt that it was this lack of testosterone that made me loathe sport and loathe the locker room culture that surrounded me at work.

Back in Potsdam, Hill was the only person to show any interest in my trip. I told him that I had been to the Baufunzel, got paralytic drunk, woke up naked, save for one black sock, slept with two East German girls and had a run in with the police. Hill smiled and said, 'Just what I would have predicted.'

I was restless. I had tasted the forbidden fruit. I had tasted neat vodka. I liked the fact that I had a secret. I was particularly pleased that I was able to tell the truth to Hill and Hill had not believed me. I could feign sincerity; what a skill! I also loved the idea of cabaret. Furthermore, I had a nagging concern that somehow, I had blighted a young East German girl's life. Eventually, I wrote a short note, thanking her for looking after me when I had drunk too much and accompanying me back to the gasthaus, as I would never have found it on my own. I asked whether her explanation to the police had satisfied them. I said that the gasthaus owner had misread the situation and I had explained the true story to him and asked him to tell the police. I translated it into German and used the DDR postal system to send the letter so as to avoid any attention from BRIXMIS. At the last minute, I folded a $100 note that I kept in my wallet for emergencies into the envelope. This was an emergency, and I had lit the blue touchpaper.

## Attachment 14

## Wistful Eye

**Caroline Jervis**

It was probably the growth on Mark's neck that changed my attitude to medicine. I realised that but for the skill of his surgeons he may well have died. Until that point, both Mother and Father had demonstrated to me that I should set my heart on any career except medicine. I was not as clever as Mark, but I was more focused. He could grasp a concept, formula or explanation and master it in seconds. He was always going to be a lawyer. I was a girl, so Mother and Father did not seem too bothered what I did. This did upset me when I thought of how difficult it had been for my mother to qualify in medicine. I did not select the university; it rather selected me, as it was my only offer. It was also the furthest from home, so I set off to Southampton and lived for my first year in a concrete block. My room was below ground level and so I had a mound in front of my window which rose up to road level.

I was that *Reading Gaol* prisoner:

*I never saw sad men who looked*
*With such a wistful eye*
*Upon that little tent of blue*
*We prisoners call the sky*
*And every happy cloud that passed*
*In such strange freedom by.*

My first year started with a bump, as I failed an important paper. It was the first exam I had ever failed, and it made me realise I had to work harder. Being in the cell helped, as there was little distraction. In one of my tutor groups was an older student. He had, by his own admission, been too cocky and overconfident in his first year and was now re-doing it as a consequence. He had some reason to be overconfident. His elder brother was a doctor of tropical medicine and had been in Malawi, and Josh had spent a year working with him before starting at Southampton. Josh had delivered babies, carried out a tracheotomy, inserted cannulae and been present at all manner of procedures that even impressed the lecturers. It did not save him from failing the first year, so he was a fine example to us all. I was probably too impressed by him and by the middle of second year, I thought he and I were "an item". His parents lived in Andover and he had been to school in Petersfield, so I quite understood that three weekends a month he would go home and would take his washing. He also played rugby for his old team and did not bother with university sport. I seldom went home as it was too far, but I would visit Mark in Oxford at every opportunity, especially as his social life seemed brilliant. Every time I went, there seemed to be a function. Josh came with me a couple of times, but he and Mark never gelled. There were no arguments nor disagreements and they both seemed to have much in common, but they just clashed.

I never got invited to anything Josh did outside university. I was living with four friends in a tidy, clean house in

Portswood, a grotty student area in Southampton. Josh lived with three men in a grotty house in Highfields, a clean and tidy area of Southampton. I was rather disappointed that Josh chose to visit his parents on the weekend of my birthday, but he bought me flowers and a rather unusual brooch, so I forgave him. I had hoped to spend some of the summer holidays with him, but he was going to visit his brother, who was back in Liverpool where he had trained. He agreed to visit me in Corton for a week but made it feel like he was doing me a favour.

The week went quite well. But on reflection, maybe I just wanted it to have gone well as it was the only week with him that summer. My father did not like him and later told me he thought him arrogant. Josh seemed indifferent to my mother. I am not sure he realised that she was also a doctor as he was rather condescending towards her.

Jenny, who was still my best friend, spent one day with us when we went rowing on the river in Durham. I asked her what she thought, as I needed someone to like him as much as I liked him.

Jenny was usually so forthright and I was surprised how guarded she was in her response. She said he was lovely and would make a fine husband for someone someday.

I asked if she meant me and she gave what I can only describe as quizzical squirm and said she hoped so, if it would make me happy. She quoted from Oscar Wilde, who she knew I adored. '*Never love anyone who treats you like you are ordinary.*'

In third year, I kept the same house but had two out of three new flatmates. Josh changed house and changed flatmates. It was to a better area but they kept it no cleaner. After one weekend up in Andover, he came back with what looked like a love-bite on his neck. I was furious with him, but he was so adamant that it was a rugby wound that I believed him. I even went into the library to do some research to see if it was plausible and it was, so I did apologise. I now know that I was increasingly dependent on him, as everything was on his terms. On weekends when he went home, I was listless, unproductive and hardly ate. Luckily, my studies were going particularly well. At half term, I did not go home but Jenny came down. Josh was back in Andover so it would work out well. Or so I thought. There is much to see and do in Southampton and Jenny and I seemed to do everything, including sailing on the Solent. The yacht was owned by the Southampton University Sailing Club and I secured places for Jenny and me to crew for a one-day sail. Neither Jenny nor I had been on a yacht, so it was a marvellous day. After being briefed by the skipper, we sailed out into the Solent, practised all the basic drills starting with man-overboard, tacking and careful jibing. It was a great experience and it was not until we were safely moored back at the marina that we really spoke of anything but sheets, winches and weather. The skipper, Dan, was a final year dental student and one of the other crew was his girlfriend Sarah, a doctor who had graduated a couple of years earlier. She was living in

Andover with her parents until she and Dan started their year travelling, planned for when Dan graduated.

Naturally, I asked Sarah if she knew the Barnes family, as big brother Leo was a doctor and Josh was well on the way to qualifying.

'Of course,' she said. 'I was at the christening.'

'Whose christening?' I asked, laughing, 'Not Josh's?'

I do not remember much of the rest of the conversation. I said that I had nausea and Jenny took me home. Jenny was so concerned that she called a taxi to deliver us back to the flat and the taxi driver asked if I needed to see a doctor.

Josh had absolutely betrayed me. He had had a double life living with a girl in Andover and had a child. What she must have felt, I shall never know. I never got to confront him. I drafted a letter which Jenny hand delivered to his flat. He never contacted me. I should have insisted he leave Southampton, but I was not strong enough. I spoke to my academic registrar and they kindly arranged for me to transfer to London to finish my studies and training. They understood my anguish but could never have felt it like I did. Jenny was wonderful and stayed almost three weeks and took care of everything. Mark came down and arranged for me to have accommodation in London with him. He had secured Articles in a London law firm. Mother and Father came down. I was not short of support but had lost the will to live. I never really picked up for several months. It was not that I was madly in love with Josh, it was just the horror, embarrassment, and the deceit.

Whether it was the Josh stress or the stress of the finals at a new university, one morning I noticed that my right eyebrow was lower than my left and the side of my mouth had slightly dropped. I did panic and thought I had had a stroke. I dialled 999 and was rushed to my own hospital. Whilst it was not a stroke, it was Bell's palsy. I was told it was temporary and after a spell on steroids, it should clear up within two to three weeks. I immediately went into full doctor research mode and found that it could last longer and, in my case, this was what happened.

Bell's palsy is no friend to anyone, especially a girl. Any slight disfigurement knocks the confidence, and it did mine. I became somewhat self-conscious and tried to present my left side to any photographer and when speaking. I avoided parties and dreaded meeting new people. When anyone was so insensitive to ask what was wrong, I explained it was Bell's palsy and that it was temporary. I suppose there was some good from my self-imposed isolation and that was I was always working and was the "go to" doctor for any crisis. Everyone could rely on Caroline, even if Caroline was damaged on the outside and broken on the inside. Mark's fiancée Francesca was beautiful, witty and clever. She was always able to bring me out of myself and I was delighted to be asked to be one of her bridesmaids, although I dreaded the photographs. I was so worried about my disfigurement that I did speak to the photographer before the wedding to ask that I always be placed on the left of the bride and groom. It was a magical wedding and I actually forgot about my face and do appear in photos from all angles.

The wedding was a chance for me to meet up with Jenny, who I had neglected after what Jenny took to calling my "Joshdown". Jenny recognised that being able to laugh about the past trauma was important and that by naming it, I could confront it. It did seem such a simple solution, but Jenny did not have to put it into action, I did, and I could not. Laughing was the last emotion I could muster.

Despite some misgivings about being almost centre stage at the wedding, I did have a wonderful day. In fact, it was the first day of our plan to put the past and Joshdown behind me. Putting the past behind me was not possible at a wedding of course, as it was all my friends from the past who gathered for the nuptials. It included my cleverest friend from university, Sheena. Sheena could do any calculation in her head faster than a calculator. She was a maths superwoman and lived with me in both the second and third year.

Sheena had once explained "game theory" to me and my other flatmates as a dating technique. It was in my early period with Josh, so I was still interested in men. Some famous mathematician, John von Neumann or John Nash, I can never remember which, had sat in a bar with three friends. They could not fail to notice that a very attractive woman had come into the bar and she too had three friends. All of Nash's clan expressed an interest in the attractive woman. Nash said if they all ignored the attractive woman and tried to chat up the others, they would all succeed. If they all focussed on the pretty one, none would succeed. Sheena then went on to explain the mathematical logic that presumably Nash had explained to his friends. This included reference to zero-sum games and perfect information. By this part of the explanation, my flatmates and I were convulsed with laughter. In the flat, terms such as "shall we go out for 'zero-sum games'" and "does anybody have any 'perfect information'" became part of our student vocabulary. Needless to say, we still use it today to tease Sheena.

After the Joshdown, I did shun anyone remotely connected with Southampton. Sadly, that included Sheena, and to a large extent, Jenny. Jenny had been too close at the crucial time and even though she had saved me, every time we met, even if Josh was not mentioned, I came away depressed. Sometimes the depression lasted for days. On one occasion, at Jenny's insistence, we walked down to the Thames. Jenny produced the brooch given to me by Josh. Jenny had taken it off my lapel on the night of the revelation. She made me throw the brooch as far as I could into the Thames. She then looked me in the eyes and said, 'Your life would have been a misery if you were still with him. He was a bastard. Now it is Caroline's time – a new epoch.'

The wedding also made me realise that I could have

lost some of my closest friends if I had continued with my self-imposed purdah.

I was delighted that at the wedding Sheena had met Geordie. He was not the accountant that I had singled out for her, but Mark told me that Geordie was in computers, so they would be very well suited. I was disappointed that I never had much chance to chat to anyone at the wedding and I never got to ask whether Geordie was still friends with the "Mark lookalike", but the chance passed.

Mark and Francesca had become enthusiastic converts to Ceroc, a French rock and roll craze that was introduced to London by a friend of a friend of Francesca. They kept trying to drag me along, but I was not quite ready to step out socially. Mark was wondering if I ever would, and although I did not tell him, I was also wondering too. It had been over four years since my face dropped and the palsy had not gone. I was trying all remedies such as different creams, exercises and even a machine that gave off electrical impulses, all to no avail.

Mark mentioned to me one day that Geordie and Sheena were now drawn into the Ceroc cult and I should come along, if only to see them. Having heard that they had been going for three weeks or more, I was concerned that they would be too far ahead. Mark said that if I wanted, he and Francesca would teach me the basic moves so that I could catch up. On this understanding, I agreed to a Tuesday evening in Wandsworth Town Hall.

The lesson with Mark and Francesca was a disaster. Mark and I had a sibling row that was the worst since we were children. He claimed I had two "gauche" feet. Luckily, Francesca stepped in and there was "entente cordiale". Further lessons were deemed unhelpful. Strangely it made me determined to go, just to show Mark how annoying his little sister could be.

I was quite excited about a night out and even changed my shift, so I was off on the Tuesday during the day and the following day as well. I did not have a large choice of what to wear, as I seldom went out. Despite having had all day, I was running late when I did finally choose an outfit. I started on make-up but just gazing at my lip started to upset me. As I looked at my make-up bag, it became crystal clear to me that I had stopped using make-up. Everything looked dried up and crusty. The mirror could not disguise the tears welling up in my eyes. I was struggling to see my eyelashes as I applied what was left of a mascara. I was all for simply not going, but I put on my best "ward round" face. I slapped on a skin tone lipstick, grabbed a bag and brolly and left the house. I was minded to walk over the bridge to Wandsworth, but it was overcast, so I jumped on a bus. I thought I would get Mark and Francesca to give me a lift home, after all I was doing this whole Ceroc thing for them.

The rain that I had predicted started to pour down in biblical proportions. I was pleased that the bus stopped outside the town hall. My brolly hardly kept off the rain but provided just enough cover to save me from the worst. I felt so sorry for the chap I ran past who was struggling to attach his bike to the railings. I was determined not to feel sorry for myself. There was always someone worse off than me and tonight he was tying his bike to a railing!

## Attachment 15

## Occam's Razor – Forward Headquarters

"Occam's Razor" was the doctrine of the mediaeval philosopher, William of Occam. Often called the law of parsimony, it states: *One should not increase, beyond what is necessary, the number of words needed to explain anything.* In 1843 after the province of Sindh had been captured following the Battle of Hyderabad, General Napier sent the one-word dispatch home, *Peccari* (*I have sinned*). Not only was Napier famed for his brevity but also his sharp wit. Mindful of his fault, George Bernard Shaw the playwright wrote to Winston Churchill, I'm *sorry this letter is so* long, I didn't have time to make it shorter.

Perhaps it is the desire to speed things up that stops people keeping it short. It is often easier to ramble on and leave nothing out that diverts us from saying what is needed. In 1836 Samuel Morse, in a groundbreaking manner, managed to speed up communication. He reduced the language into dots and dashes with his simple code. Everyone knows; *dit dit dit – dah dah dah – dit dit dit (SOS)* and it has, as a consequence saved lives.

But the victor ludorum (the winner of the contest) of brachylogy must go to Victor Hugo. He wanted to know how the sales of the newly released *Les Miserables* were going. He telegraphed his publisher:

?

The reply was:

!


### *Brigadier Pardue CBE RA (ret'd)*

*Those who have read Les Miserables know that there is a full chapter which gives a vivid description of the Battle of Waterloo. Some historians go as far as to say it is one of the most accurate depictions of what happened at Waterloo, even though it is woven into a work of fiction. Therefore, apologies for this poor explanation of NATO and the role of British forces in Germany, it is as short as possible.*

*The North Atlantic Treaty Organisation (NATO) was established in 1949 by the Western Allies with a simple doctrine that an attack on any one country was an attack on them all. If the great Soviet Bear was to attack across the wide north German plain, the NATO allies, of which Great Britain was one, would be ready to confront any threat and repel any aggression.*

*Catterick Barracks was in Bielefeld, West Germany and the headquarters of the 1st British Corps. There were four divisions in the corps and three of the divisions were in West Germany. The fourth, "2nd Division", was based in the United Kingdom but deployed to West Germany in the event of any threat from the Soviet Union. The plucky four divisions of the 1st British Corps would hold fast on various rivers which ran helpfully south to north across the said north German plain.*

*The first river that would halt the Soviet attack was the River Weser and it flowed right through the centre of the 1st British Corps' area of responsibility. This river is best known from the poem, The Pied Piper of Hamelin, but for the British Military, it was a main obstacle to any plan by the Soviets to launch an attack into the heart of Western Europe. The Weser was probably the easiest river to cross at any point, as it had countless bridges.*

*In the event of hostilities, friendly troops had to get forward and over the river to stop the Soviets but if they were overwhelmed, the same troops would need the same bridges for their retreat, a retreat being more appropriately described by the military as a "tactical withdrawal". Given that in conflict, the routes to the bridges could be blocked by civilians, much of the military planning was about bridges. On the outbreak of any conflict, many bridges would simply be destroyed by 1st British Corps. But some would not. Some would be designated main civilian routes, and some would be main supply routes. Depending on how well the defences were holding up, the generals running the battle would decide how each bridge was dealt with. Many were essential and called reserve demolitions. They were prepared for demolition but not actually blown until ordered from the highest level. Bridges were very, very important.*

*There are two levels of secret higher than "Top Secret". In Catterick Barracks, the list of the reserve demolition bridges on the Weser were the very highest level of secrecy. The defence of the bridges and the knowledge of which bridges were to be guarded and which were to be destroyed was entrusted to 2nd Division. The second or Keystone Division, had its headquarters in York. It had a small forward headquarters in Catterick Barracks in Bielefeld. The headquarters cell consisted of a handful of staff officers with highly vetted civilian support. One secretary worked in a Faraday cage, typing and promulgating information. The cage stopped any electronic eavesdropping.*

*It wasn't all work in Catterick Barracks, the healthy minds needed healthy bodies. The annual sports trophy, played for by all branches and departments, was the Coe Cup. Some hapless junior staff officer was nominated to organise and timetable all the events. If the Coe Cup was a success, the staff officer's career was safe. If it was a disaster, the staff officer's career was holed below the water line.*

*It was on a Coe Cup day, when the whole of the headquarters was involved in some sport or other, that the secretary in 2nd Inf Division forward headquarters copied from three eight-inch floppy discs the details of the reserve demolition bridges onto three spare eight-inch floppy discs. She told the staff officer who had instructed her to make some minor amendments to the original discs that the task had been completed. She asked if the computer could be shut down. He gratefully thanked her for her speed and efficiency. He completed the register, which recorded the original removal of the top-secret discs from the safe; to note that they had been returned. He then returned the precious discs to the safe. He carefully scrambled the dial and had one check of the large lever handle to confirm it was closed. He then shouted through to the secretary, 'Auf wiedersehen,' and rushed off to his hockey match.*

*The secretary placed her copy discs in a tennis racket cover. She carefully locked the Faraday cage door and walked out of the office, which she also locked, and she went down the stairs to the exit. Just before the iron clad security doors, she handed in her keys to the internal key co-ordinator on reception. At the iron clad security door, she simply made a tennis shot gesture towards the guard who dodged the imaginary ball. The Brigadier needs his racket she mouthed, and she was waived through.*

*The secretary was not a spy, and she did not even know what she was going to do with the discs. She did know her husband was a cheat and if anyone was going to bugger up his Army career, it would be her, not some floozy from the language school. No one from the headquarters even knew the discs were missing and never would, save for the usual, unusual turn of events.*

## Attachment 16

## Drowning

**Gordon Shawcross**

I struggled to lock my bike. My hands were cold and dripping wet. Rain was rushing down my back and into my trousers. My keys were a blur as the rain washed down through my hair. I just abandoned the bike. No one would be stupid enough to be out on a night like this stealing bikes and if they were, I thought they could have it. I could hear my feet squelching in my shoes as I went into the entrance. Various people were milling about. Some were shaking off umbrellas, hats and waterproof clothing. All were damp but none were drowned, that is, save for me.

I could not see Sheena or Geordie, and everyone seemed to be gazing at me, probably wondering how one person could have such a large pool of water under them without a hose or a bucket. The elastic band round my ankle had stopped the oily chain marking my trousers but had acted as a stopper on a drain. My left trouser leg was full of water. When I snapped the elastic band, a gush of more water flooded onto the floor. I saw that there was a queue to hand in coats at a table. As I looked up, everyone in the queue was smiling or should I say laughing at me. Beyond the table, there were the toilets. I toyed with heading to them for sanctuary but then decided that I would just leave and catch a taxi or bus home. I was embarrassed by the pool on the floor and thought I should at least try and mop it up before leaving, but the pool was getting bigger. I looked down at my dripping feet and that confirmed my position. I would just cycle home. I turned to leave when a girl said, 'So you are so keen on Ceroc that you swam the Thames to get here?'

I lifted my head to look at the girl, but another rush of water came from my hair down and down my face. I sort of recognised the girl through the blur and I mumbled about having no change of clothes and nothing dry, so I was just leaving.

The girl remonstrated with me and said, 'We can find things for you.'

Almost on cue, the helper from the cloakroom came over and said in a French accent, 'Here are some overalls from the janitor cupboard. Put them on until you dry out.' Maybe because the chap seemed authoritarian or simply that my brain was washed out, but I did his bidding. Moments later, I found myself entering, with bare feet, a huge dance hall, full of people. I was dressed in a blue Wandsworth Town Hall janitor's jumpsuit. It took Sheena and Geordie at least twenty minutes to stop laughing at me and they started again when Mark and Francesca arrived. I was offered some black brogues by a man who had come from the office and changed into his dancing shoes. It seemed so generous that I couldn't refuse. They were far too tight, but I thought that at least they would give my feet some protection when the dancing ordeal started.

I could probably have lived with the shame and embarrassment of the evening by never seeing anyone again, had it not been for the fact that the girl I spoke to at the entrance turned out to be Mark's sister Caroline. Caroline came over to join Geordie and Sheena and was introduced more formally to me by Sheena through her giggles. Caroline had laughed but did see my discomfort. I did love her laugh, as one side of her mouth was just slightly lower than the other and it made her so attractive. Everyone commented on how I looked so much like Mark. They all went on to joke that they could tell us apart because Mark was not wearing a blue jump suit!

Caroline did know some of the other "Cerocers" or whatever the term was, but seemed unattached. I found myself increasingly left with her and it rather pleased me, notwithstanding my tight shoes and ridiculous outfit. Caroline recalled the "orange party" and apologised for her father and mother's behaviour.

I reminded her that we were just kids and it was a decade and a half ago. Caroline hugged my arm, just like she had at the party so long ago. The flashback was uncanny but this time I found myself putting my spare arm up so my hand could touch her shoulder. I was then saying almost without thinking, 'You are not getting away this time so easily – if anyone shouts, just ignore them.' Caroline and I sat out a couple of dances and then enjoyed the last together. We neither of us knew the moves but were happy in our own embrace. Mark was dropping Caroline off in Putney but not before Caroline and I exchanged numbers and agreed to meet the following night in the Sloany Pony, the local name for the White Horse on Putney Heath.

My clothes were still dripping, despite two hours on the town hall radiator. I abandoned any idea of getting my socks on and left them along with my underpants in a wastepaper basket. Heaven knows what the cleaner would think. The ride home was cold and uncomfortable, but at least it was direct, unlike the journey to Albert Mansions. I was also riding on air. I was not sure what sensation was coursing through my veins, as I had not experienced it before, but I put it down as *love*. I even had it in capital letters in my thoughts. Caroline and I met the next night and the following night and I had no idea of what we talked about, what we ate or where we went. My life was predictable, but Caroline's was governed by shifts and rotas that changed constantly. She was unable to see me on the Friday or Saturday during the day but agreed to meet Saturday night and we further arranged to meet with Sheena and Geordie for lunch on the Sunday.

On the Saturday evening, Caroline and I cut the

evening short as Caroline had worked all day and was feeling tired. I had a mild panic that she was going off me and felt my insecurities rising. We sat on a bench near Putney Bridge Station for a last time together before I was planning to catch the Tube to Tooting Bec, my nearest station. Caroline rested her head on my shoulder. She had a tear in her left eye and I instinctively dabbed it with my handkerchief. Caroline stood up abruptly and brushed away my hand. I was startled and surprised. Caroline sat down, crying, 'Sorry, sorry.' She wept. I put my arm back round her shoulders.

I thought, *Oh damn, she is going to finish with me*. I found my eyes watering. I asked her if it was something I had said or done that had upset her. There was a long pause which simply fed my exploding insecurity. Then Caroline confessed that she was still sensitive to the Bell's palsy. I expressed genuine bafflement as I had no idea what Bell's palsy was.

Caroline said, 'Look at this,' pointing to her eye. 'Can't you see the droop?'

I replied that I could, but had not thought it anything and it did not detract from her beauty. Caroline started crying again and hugged me so tightly, I was taken unawares and gasped. I was crying too. We both laughed and Caroline hugged me again and gave me a long kiss. Caroline explained Bell's palsy to me in more detail and the anxiety it had caused her over the years.

I explained that I'd thought she was going to end our relationship! This made her cry even more and I too was overcome so we had to share the hankie.

We walked to the Tube and Caroline said that she wished I could come back with her as she did not want to leave me.

In an unusually quick response for me, I suggested that as it was early, we could take a taxi to Streatham and I could pick up a change of clothes then we could come back. So it was that Caroline and I ended up having breakfast together on Sunday morning in Putney.

### Attachment 17

### Honour

**A P Stein**

Whilst I was still feeling somewhat vulnerable because of my lapse of standards, as time went on, I felt better that I had at least dealt with the whole "Inge matter" in an honourable manner. After almost six months I had hoped that the incident was behind me, but it was not to be so. Post was always sporadic to the mission, and everyone knew that they could not send any secure correspondence, as it would be read by the Stasi, so I was surprised to receive what appeared to be an unopened letter from Leipzig. It was not from Inge as expected, but from Thorsten. It started *Lieber Affe*, which amused me. Thorsten expressed how sorry he had been for not joining Inge and I for breakfast, which resulted in her arrest. He felt if he, Thorsten, had been with us, the misunderstanding could never have occurred. Thorsten went on to acknowledge the kind gift to Inge but noted she was accepting on behalf of all of them, as she did not want to be seen to be taking money from me, given the background to the "gift".

    I thought, *What a decent group of people these were*. Thorsten went on to say that they had all had a wonderful evening at the kabarett and that I should return again. Inge had been reprimanded for her actions and what had amused Inge and her friends was that the police had asked her if she wanted to join the Stasi! Seemingly the Stasi had a catalogue of requirements "between 20 and 30, unmarried, no children, foreign language skills, good-looking, educated, analytical skills and patriotism". They had all laughed as Inge had all the qualities, but they joked that she was not good looking.

I felt so uplifted by the letter and whilst I never got back to Leipzig, I did continue to correspond with Thorsten and, occasionally, Klaus and Inge. I also included a dollar note, usually $100, because I could, but it was also an incentive for them to reply.

After the Leipzig trip I reported what I had seen to London. I mentioned the people I had met but did not dwell on the circumstances. London was delighted by the depth of information I was able to impart. Some seven months later, and just a month before I was to be moved back to London, I was approached by Sergei. It was after a commemoration service for something. I had long stopped taking too much interest in the actual events, as they adopted the same traditional format. Sergei started off by saying how grateful he was for yet more King Edward cigars that I had given to him and he now wanted to repay the longstanding friendship between us. Sergei had been told he too was due to leave his post, as he was returning to St Petersburg. He wanted to leave Potsdam a happier place.

I was perplexed, as I did not think two years was longstanding and friendship did seem an overstatement but I smiled and played along. 'Things are changing in Russia,' Sergei almost lectured me. 'Gorbachev is different, soon it will all be different. No more Chernobyl, more glasnost.' Sergei lapsed into Russian to use the word for "openness". He proceeded to tell me exactly what he had been told about my trip to Leipzig. He never said when he had been told, nor exactly what he had been told, but he alluded to my night of "mischief". He clearly had not been appraised of the full story, as he believed I had been blackmailed by an East German girl. I did not correct him, especially when he went on to say how much he despised the Stasi and their primitive tricks. He and I embraced. Sergei's final words to me were, 'Do not worry about the Stasi. They are the common enemy.' He growled as he pretended to spit. 'Your secret is safe with me.'

Sergei was right about the mood-music in Eastern Europe. Poland had been simmering with independent thought and actions for almost a decade. I thought that if Sergei had half the story on Leipzig, the Stasi could have so much more. Whilst I never lost the niggle that I had been compromised on the night in Hohne Strasse, none of my dealings with Inge or the flat friends had caused any concerns. I took a bold decision and decided to tell London the full story on my return. I was at pains never to lie but I was careful not to reveal everything. My main line of disclosure was that I had been on a bender after the church and had gone on to a nightclub and stayed over with a crowd of German friends. I did not say how much of the night I had forgotten. London behaved uncharacteristically. They said that my contacts had proved helpful beyond measure and that all the simmering discontent in East Germany was based on the St Nicholas Church in Leipzig. I was fêted in London and was to return on promotion. I was surprised to hear that it was my ability to act so unexpectedly that had changed perceptions of me, especially amongst the uniformed element in the Ministry. I presumed that if the SERBs knew, Sergei knew, the Stasi knew and Hill knew, it was not such a secret. I was to enter the MOD stratosphere and it had been fuelled by one night of vodka and cabaret. I vowed that there would be more nights like it in the future.

# Attachment 18

## Routine

**A P Stein**

On return to London, I occupied the family flat in Chelsea. It had been owned by my parents and, as the eldest son, I acquired it simply because my sister was not interested in it. I took to returning to Frome on a Saturday morning and coming back to London on a Monday morning. It worked well for Jocasta, as she could attend church on Sunday morning and if the twins did not want to join her, I could step in. I enjoyed the girls' company, they would call me second Pa or PaPa and Jocasta MaMa and we would visit places of attraction together, such as Westonbirt Arboretum or the Cheddar Gorge.

During the week in London, I created a fairly rigid regime that included at least one meal a week at my club in St James. This was a necessary evil if I was to reach the highest office which I increasingly coveted. My one vice was cabaret. Cabaret had replaced Mendelssohn as my release. Every Friday, I would head to the West End and visit a cabaret club. At first, I was self-conscious and would only stay a short period. I would only go to clubs where I felt comfortable. I rejected some as they were seedy, others because I felt threatened and others simply because the quality of the shows was poor. Amongst my comprehensive reading during the week would be *Time Out*, the listing magazine. I was both surprised and pleased that there were so many cabaret and burlesque clubs in and around London. Burlesque clubs were slightly more risqué than the cabaret clubs, but all the clubs had more things in common than separated them. I found myself drawn to one club more than any other and it became my "regular". Quentin, the show director, became a nodding acquaintance and then almost a friend. I started to be recognised and Gino, the head barman, would often try and have a vodka and orange waiting for me as I arrived. The Bohemian, the club, combined all the best features that I enjoyed. Good show, convivial atmosphere and appreciative audience. I had been to too many clubs where the clientele was there to drink and who ignored the show. I was never able to work out the cause and effect. *If the show improved, would the clientele improve or vice versa?*

I started to write up notes as a diary on each club visit. I had no idea why, but I considered submitting reviews to *Time Out*. I never did, but rather like my coin collection and my stamp collection, the reviews became my new hobby. Heaven knows what the Ministry would think. I kept the notes in a leather sleeve cover designed for the *Radio Times*. I had two of them which I had inherited with the flat and as I did not watch television, they were surplus to requirements but too good to discard.

The Bohemian always seemed to be trying to provide the best show possible. I did notice when the club employed a master of ceremonies. Until then, the leading lady who opened the show and closed it would "sort of" introduce the acts. The new fellow was tall, good looking and had some talent. I had thought the shows were better for having the continuity offered by the new man. I told Quentin of this observation and Quentin had said it had been his idea and he too thought it worked. Quentin had also pointed out that he valued my opinion, especially when he found out that I was familiar with almost every cabaret bar from London and Leipzig. I mentioned that I kept a note on each of the shows I visited but that it was just because it was the perfect distraction from my normal life, not for any other purpose.

It had not surprised me when the young MC came over and spoke to me one night, seeking comment on the show. The chap tried to suggest that it was a survey of customers but he had bought me a vodka and orange, so I knew I had been singled out. I initially introduced myself as AP and then changed it to Affe. On a whim I adopted my "German cabaret name".

The MC introduced himself as Sean and then when I suddenly changed, he too switched and said, 'Jaffa is my longstanding nickname.' We both laughed. With this in common, Affe and Jaffa as we became, spent at least ten, increasing to twenty and then thirty, minutes each Friday night chatting.

Whilst much of the conversation was about burlesque, both found it amusing to break into Russian and German, particularly to confuse eavesdroppers. I liked Jaffa's company and I felt that this was reciprocated.

## Attachment 19

## Musca (The Fly)

### Quentin McCrae

Children with parents who wear uniform are, I presume, usually proud of them. A dad in the police or the Royal Marines or a mum as a nurse fits many a stereotype for most people in their formative years and it did for me. Sadly, I was not proud, I was embarrassed. My mother and father were in the Salvation Army. I now look back fondly on the Christmas band concerts and the actual church services, but I cringe when I think of the sports days or parent nights when they arrived in uniform. Uniform for them meant they fitted in, for me it meant I stood out. I am grateful that I learnt the cornet and could sing, but I never talk of my legacy. My mother was, if nothing, a brave and committed Christian and I recognise that now but I did not at the time. She famously went into WH Smith bookshop in Chesterfield and pre-ordered *Lady Chatterley's Lover* when publication was allowed by the High Court. When it arrived, she went with her band and collected it. She never touched it but held it in oven gloves. She then set fire to it in the street. The incident gained some notoriety and it was never forgotten by neighbours and school friends and certainly never forgotten by me. I realised that there was more fun in that book than there was in the religion.

I am Quentin McCrae but I was not a Quentin or in fact a McCrae. I am one of the many journeyman actors/directors/stagehands that are essential to the West End. We all aspire to the bright lights and fame but most of us end up having a nine to five existence and in my case, it had been nine at night until five in the morning. I had not always been in the performing arts. After school I went to catering college and then cooked on a ship taking "ten pound poms" to Australia. I jumped ship in Hong Kong for no reason, save that it was the first city I had seen since Chesterfield and it was awesome.

Ship companies found it easy to find cooks and crew in the far east, but they struggled to find entertainers. I realised that there was more fun and better pay if I did some bugling, singing and dancing. My small-town Chesterfield talent would never have transferred to the bright lights, but they were more than adequate for cruise liners. I was able to survive and prosper singing in a backing group called The Flies. There were four or five of us, depending on the availability and we had various singers to support, most of whom changed with each cruise. Sometimes we were Micky Flynn and The Flies but we could well be Cynthia Smith and The Flies or Rock Marsden and The Flies, depending on who had been booked as the singer. I was able to say that the happiest time of my life was with The Flies in Hong Kong.

*I also found time to read and write and to learn. I reinvented myself as Quentin McCrae. I found I could be as good, or as bad, at whatever I did, as I wanted to be.*

On one drunken run ashore in Macau, we - me, and the four other Flies - had tattoos. We decided that we needed a "fly" permanently inked onto our bodies. This would not have been unusual, except that we had them on the flat area of skin behind our scrotums. We agreed that this was the least likely place for a tattoo and would only ever be seen at our post-mortems. Perhaps it was the twenty minutes of pain or the shared absurdity, but we all agreed that it bonded us like no other brotherhood in the world. We pledged, over another round of post-tattoo drinks, that the brotherhood would meet at least once a year for the rest of our lives. In fact, the brotherhood only met once since those youthful days and that was when Rick, the oldest and most sensible, was married in Weston-super-Mare. After the ceremony, all five of us Flies gathered at the reception. Whilst we were not quite as drunk as we had been on the night in Macau, we gathered in the gents' cloakroom to release the flies. This was the dropping of the trousers and the lifting of the leg in a sumo wrestler pose. It was such fun until the Bishop of Truro, who had been officiating at the wedding, walked in.

I never tired of telling this story. Sean had always wanted to know if it was true but one of the rules of the brotherhood was that the fly would never be released except to other Flies or next-of-kin.

When I returned from the Far East, I stumbled into the burlesque scene, first as a drag artiste. I was Lady Beth Macbeth. It was an inspirational choice, as the act made much of Shakespeare's language spoken by the anti-heroine; unsex me here; out, damned spot; look like the innocent flower but be the serpent under't. I never really noticed that the intellectual and literary qualities of the act were lost on most customers, but it was just enough input to make people think I was well educated and maybe even classically trained. The whole life of a performer is an act. I just kept trying to improve my performance, and in doing so, improve my life.

I was not born great; I certainly had not had greatness thrust upon me and so I had to achieve greatness. When the original burlesque artistic director was removed from the Bohemian Club on a stretcher, I was a struggling third string act, but I stepped up to organise everybody. No-one else was interested or were only interested in themselves, which made my job easy. The original director never sobered up enough to return and I shed my frock and became the show director by default. I learnt that there was little money for investment in the show. Rents were high, competition was strong, and customers were not loyal. I was sober and I was enthusiastic. What better qualities could the Bohemian have asked for?

I was delighted by the impact Sean was having on the club. The show seemed so much more complete and I have to say that I took some pride for introducing this innovation. As I wallowed in self-congratulation, I did puzzle as to the circumstances of Sean's arrival, as he had been imposed on me. At the time I had wondered if Sean was the son of the owner or had some other influential friend. I had raised the issue with Steve, the Manager because I was indignant that my artistic discretion was being fettered. Steve was non-plussed and said he would raise the point, but he never did. I was "bought off" by an increase in the budget and an assurance that the owner wanted to take the establishment upmarket. I was also given an assurance that the club could close at the end of March for two weeks for at least a re-paint. This tied in with my long-harboured plan to develop the club. I had, until this time, done nothing. I had noticed the improved quality of the clientele and I found more time to think as I had less time to worry. I even re-started my scrapbook that I had neglected since Hong Kong. Sean and I were fellow lovers of Shakespeare and thought alike. The show could be wonderful and I decided that I could make Sean Cross a star. A dusted off, long forgotten show that I had written for Lady Beth Macbeth called *The Shaming of the Few*. I knew that *West Side Story* was based on *Romeo and Juliet* - why couldn't I do something similar? My imagination went into overdrive. I decided I was going to meet with the owner. I had a plan.

## Attachment 20

## Duets

**Ryan Haston (Sean Cross)**

I was loving life. The show was getting better, I was growing in confidence and that meant my ad-libbing seemed more natural, my jokes were better received and the other acts appreciated my introductions and perfect timing. The whole show was working so well. Quentin had moved from the shadows, where he would once have sat with his head in his hands, to a table front left. The established clientele was more numerous and spent more at the bar. Gino and the bar staff were delighted. Their tips improved. All involved put the success down to my work as the Master of Ceremonies.

I had befriended Stein, who I called Affe, after he explained the background to the incorrect translation of his German name. Stein called me Jaffa. We spoke mainly about Shakespeare and burlesque but would often lapse into Russian and German, usually to tell private jokes or gossip about someone. I was hating my temporary accommodation and I had thought of going back to Lela's but I had been told to use the digs offered. This did puzzle me. It was worse accommodation and whilst it was not costing me anything, it was just round the corner from Lela's. I was minded to raise this with

Robert, but he had kept a low profile, so I did not want to prod the bear.

Quentin had asked me to sing a duet with the chanteuse and it had worked so well that Quentin suggested I opened the show with *Wilkommen* from *Cabaret*. I had never considered myself a singer, except for rugby songs, but I could hold a tune. Quentin was confident that provided I did not try and emulate Joel Grey who sang in the film, I would be fine. I mentioned to Stein, on the Friday night that I was planning to have my own opening number from *Cabaret* but had never seen the film. Stein told me that he was able to remedy that. Stein had the video and was happy to host a *Cabaret* night at his flat.

I was to have my first introduction to Embankment Gardens. We chose the Monday evening, which was my night off. I caught a Tube to Sloane Square, changing at South Kensington. Stein had obviously gone to great lengths to make the evening work. Even though it was a February night, he had cooked bratwurst on a small barbecue situated on his small, decked terrace. Stein had deep fried frites and had mayo and curry powder just like a Schnellimbis, a German fast-food outlet. The beer was German and we drank out of steins. Stein explained to me that the theme was in bad taste if taken in context of the film. Stein explained it was just that "a theme" and he was, or at least used to be, Jewish. I never quite understood what he meant, as I always assumed you were just born into a religion and that was that. The film was terrific and when it was finished, we replayed the opening number at least ten times and sang heartily.

Stein brought the evening to a close by explaining to me that he had a meeting with the Minister in the morning. He explained that Ministers only worked a three-day week in Westminster. I joked that it was the type of job I wanted. He said that there were two bedrooms and that I could stay, but I was minded that I wanted to be in control of the whole situation and declined. Whilst sitting on a cold damp Sloane Square Tube station waiting for the last Tube, I thought I had made the wrong decision. I cheered myself up by singing the song that would open the show. It turned a few heads, but most smiled.

## Attachment 21

## Duets

**A P Stein**

On the following Friday, I was delighted to hear Jaffa open the show with the tune that he and I had learnt together. Jaffa had a great voice and though he was not a singer, he did carry off the ceremony of the act well. After the show, Jaffa singled me out and we were joined by Quentin, who was ecstatic. Quentin ordered a bottle of Moet & Chandon and Gino brought it over. Quentin made Gino join the group and we all toasted a very successful night. Jaffa explained that it was me that had taught him the song. Quentin mistook the statement and assumed I had taught him to sing. Quentin then spent the next hour persuading me to teach him more and suggested various songs that would suit Jaffa. Neither Jaffa nor I put the record straight but we did agree, in Russian, to meet on Sunday evening to watch a video. I suggested, also in Russian, that Jaffa brought a weekend bag and stayed over.

I had a busy week at the office and the Jaffa evening was on me before I knew it. The result was that I almost failed to grab any film. I had stopped at the Blockbuster on the King's Road just as they were locking up to close.

The till had already been switched off, but the shop assistant was happy to take a fifty pound note off me for the two musicals. He couldn't give a receipt or change but I was happy to have grabbed anything in the circumstances. So it was that Affe and Jaffa met and watched *Grease*. It was that or *Oklahoma!*. I went back to the West Country for the weekend, leaving Jaffa. I told him he was welcome to stay as long as he liked and he seemed content.

## Attachment 22

## Cabaret

**Ryan Haston**

I did stay over in Stein's spare room. I had lost some sleep the previous night as to how I would react if he suggested we share a bed. Stein was married but in the West End scene, that did not seem to matter. Robert, my so-called minder who put me up to this had asked whether I was comfortable with homosexuality and I was, but I was not sure if Stein was homosexual. I was not sure I was straight. I was not aroused by the girls at the theatre, even when they were half naked in the dressing rooms. I was popular and was often propositioned but I always declined. I told myself that it was unprofessional to "screw the crew". Most of the females assumed I was gay, but none of the men did or at least those I knew to be gay never propositioned me. I was not particularly attracted to men either. I took to calling myself retro-sexual when the subject came up. This meant I could explain anything to anybody and they would not be any the wiser. It would not have worked on my father; if I had told him I was not interested in girls, he would have just insisted I was interested in men; there could be no middle ground. In the event, the situation never arose at the flat. Stein and I enjoyed the film and next day walked along the embankment and had brunch overlooking the river.

Stein had decided to change his commute routine to return to Frome midweek to attend a school function with Jocasta, so he had the extra day in London. Stein never asked me to move in but he never asked me to leave and after a couple of weeks I was Stein's lodger. Stein worked late and I worked even later, so the two of us seldom met.

Stein had told Jocasta of me, his new flatmate, and she seemed quite relaxed and this put my mind at rest. All I was missing was my bike. I wanted to recover my Brompton and various clothes from Lela. Life was good.

Stein had a comprehensive library at the flat and I found I had an hour every day before I went to work when I could sit back and read. The reading was eclectic and varied from philosophy to Russian novels. I particularly liked to read the bundles that Stein kept in two leather folders designed for the *Radio Times*. One contained all Stein's notes on cabaret and burlesque. It was bursting at the seams but contained some really interesting information. Stein was a natural writer. The second bundle could not have been more of a contrast. It was the daily non-classified Ministry of Defence reports that summarised events around the world. Stein would gather the sheets weekly and bind them into the folder. Stein had no television as such. He had a screen to watch videos but had never thought to have an aerial. He also had an extensive library of records. I would put Mendelssohn's *Violin concerto in E minor* on in the background and browse through his books for an hour.

One evening, my attention was drawn to an article in the MOD brief of the return to the Soviet Union of a Soviet national for behaviour "inconsistent" with her visa. Seemingly, the girl, a ballerina, had been in England to study and had been compromised whilst working for persons unknown in Cheltenham. What caught my eye was the fact that the girl hailed from Neeme, 40 km north of Tallin, and that she had entered the country legally. Her name was redacted, as was another sentence. I made a mental note to raise this with Stein. I then thought better of it. Stein may not approve of me reading the revelations in the *Radio Times* binder. I did go to work that evening more troubled than I should have been. Notwithstanding my concerns, they were washed away by the performance. The show was terrific and I thought nothing more of it. Quentin wanted me to learn *Sag mir wo die Blumen Sind* which had been a hit for Marlene Dietrich. Quentin gave me a green flimsy folder of sheet music for the music and lyrics. I spoke German, so the lyrics were fine but I had no idea about the tune. It was Stein who came to my rescue.

Stein recognised the song *Where have all the flowers gone?* It had been a popular tune for the Searchers in the 1960s, so with Stein's humming and my singing, we were able to rehearse. Stein said that the music would not have been his choice as it was too "pop", as he described it.

Stein said *Mack the Knife* would have been better.

I thought that *Mack the Knife* was also "pop", and told him so. Stein proceeded to educate me.

He said, 'Not in the original German.' The original version was from *The Threepenny Opera* and the play opens with the Moritat singer comparing Macheath (*Mack the Knife*) with a shark and then telling tales of his crimes: arson, robbery, rape and murder.

'Well that sounds fun,' I suggested. I used the chance to say that I had seen Stein's notes in the *Radio Times* folder on cabaret. I was sure he would have no issue with me reading them and I hoped I could then raise the issue of Neeme in the other folder.

Stein simply said, 'Yes, I had meant to ask you to read my notes.' Stein picked up the folder from beside the sofa and extracted a page. 'Here,' he said, 'is my opening chapter.' Neeme was relegated and I settled down to read.

*The term kabarett originally it is believed from Middle Dutch. The first time found in print of the word kabarett is a document from 1275 to mean an inexpensive inn or restaurant.*

*Kabaretts had appeared in Paris by at least the late fifteenth century. They were different to taverns because they served food as well as wine. Kabaretts were considered better than taverns; the tables were covered with cloth, and the price was charged by the plate, not the mug. They were not specifically centres of entertainment but musicians were known to perform there. By the end of the sixteenth century, they were the preferred place to dine out. In the seventeenth century, a clearer distinction emerged when taverns were limited to selling wine, and later to serving full wholesome meals.*

*Cabarets as they became known were often gathering places for writers artists and actors. Moliere and Jean Racine were known to frequent a cabaret called the Mouton Blanc.*

*In 1773, French poets, painters, musicians and writers began to meet in a cabaret called Le Caveau, where they sang bawdy songs that they had written. The Caveau continued until 1816, when it was forced to close because its clients wrote songs mocking the Royal Family.*

*The first modern cabaret was probably the Le Chat Noir in Montmartre, which was the bohemian neighbourhood of Paris, and it was established in 1881 by a theatrical agent and entrepreneur to combine music and other entertainment with political commentary and satire. The Chat Noir brought together the wealthy and famous of Paris with the bohemians and artists of Montmartre, its clientele a mixture of writers and painters, of journalists and students, of employees and high-rollers, as well as models, prostitutes and true grandes dames searching for exotic experiences. The Master of Ceremonies called himself a gentleman-cabaretier. He began each show with a monologue mocking the wealthy, ridiculing the members of the French Parliament, and making satirical topical jokes.*

*By 1896, there were fifty-six cabarets and cafés with music in Paris, along with a dozen music halls. The cabarets did not have a good reputation; one critic wrote in 1897 that "they sell drinks worth fifteen centimes along with verses which, for the most part, are worth nothing." By the end of the century, there were only a few cabarets of the old style remaining where artists and bohemians gathered.*

*The music hall, first invented in London, appeared in Paris in 1862. It offered more lavish musical and theatrical productions, with elaborate costumes, singing and dancing. The theatres of Paris, fearing competition from the music halls, had a law passed by the National Assembly forbidding music hall performers to wear costumes, dance, wear wigs, or recite dialogue. The law was challenged by the owner of the music hall Eldorado in 1867, who put a former famous actress on stage to recite verse from Corneille and Racine. The public took the side of the music halls, and the law was repealed.*

*The Moulin Rouge was a striking building s opened in 1889. It had a huge red windmill on its roof. It was to gain most fame as the home of the new French dance known as the Can-can. It was helped by the quality of the acts which was to include singers that became world famous such as Mistinguett and Édith Piaf. The posters for the venue were painted by Henri Toulouse-Lautrec, In the 20th century, the competition from the film industry meant that these dance halls put on performances that were increasingly more spectacular. The Folies Bergère, which had been founded in 1869, competed with The Moulin Rouge as its great rival. Its stars in the 1920s included the American singer and dancer Josephine Baker.*

*German kabarett was active from the beginning of the 1900s, with the start of the Überbrettl (Superstage) venue, and by the Weimar Republic from 1925 onwards, the kabarett shows were filled with withering political satire and a humour that was intended to shock. It was similar to the French cabaret in the small friendly and convivial surroundings but the shock and politics were peculiar to Germany.*

*Le Lido on the Champs-Élysées opened just after the Second World War with singers such as Édith Piaf, Marlene Dietrich, and Maurice Chevalier, but it also included acts such as Laurel & Hardy. The Famous Crazy Horse Saloon which included strip-tease did not open until the 1950s.*

I never realised just how committed this middle-aged civil servant was to such a diverse art form. I told Stein how impressed I was in having such an interesting "flatmate". Stein was somewhat embarrassed by my praise. I should have raised the issue of Marta from Neeme but the moment slipped and I did not want to raise it cold.

I had inherited my father's Rolex Oyster Perpetual Bubbleback. I used to think that I was fonder of my watch than I was of my father. The watch was a cause of much of my anxiety as I never knew whether I was safer wearing it or hiding it, especially when I was working. I mentioned this anxiety to Stein and he suggested I put the watch on his household insurance policy. I agreed and he asked me if I wanted to keep it in the safe at the flat and I was delighted to do so. He asked if there was anything else of value and so I also put my passport and my leather folder containing my degree certificate and some other bits, that had no value, but I would have been sad to lose. I added the sheet music to *Willkommen*, a landmark in my developing career, to my folder. I was still troubled by Marta, but at least my watch was secure.

## Attachment 23

## Tuva Tannu

**A P Stein**

About four weeks after Jaffa had moved in, we had the first night when we were both home early and our clocks were in alignment. We decided on another night of comic opera and I must confess I had too many vodkas. I had gone to bed early, but I was nursing a headache the next morning. I was called to Tuesday morning Minister's prayers, hoping I could keep a low profile. It was the gathering where the civil servants and the uniformed high command would meet and follow a predetermined agenda to brief the Minister. I had a mild hangover but was pleased that I had had such a good night.

The agenda, as was most agenda across all government departments at that time, was the growing threat of AIDS. A campaign had been launched headed "Don't Die of Ignorance". The Minister was keen that all military personnel had free access to condoms. There was much discussion on homosexuality in the armed forces, as it was perceived that the gay community was most vulnerable to what had been originally labelled "the gay plague". Homosexuality was banned in the armed forces and the Minister was adamant that service personnel should be warned of the dangers of any promiscuity. I was mindful of how careful all those who spoke "chose their words". This was not a topic that any of the gathered throng were comfortable with. One of the ministerial aides noted that I shared a flat with a young man. I was shocked by the untimely intervention but stayed focussed. I chose to say nothing, which I knew was counterintuitive, as I wanted to scream that the young man was my lodger. My silence put the aide firmly in the spotlight.

He spluttered that it was not relevant and apologised. This had the effect of making him look even more foolish. I knew that he would not have raised the point unless he had been directed by the Minister, so I chose my words carefully.

I said that I was more than happy to show my support for the homosexual community and I for one would welcome a more enlightened approach to homosexuals in the armed forces. I added that I was happily married but had a flat in London for use during the week and I did indeed have a lodger.

The Minister thanked me for my contribution and said he hoped all those at the meeting would be as open about their views.

After the meeting, I was approached by one of the brigadiers from the intelligence section with whom I occasionally worked on briefing papers. At this level of command, one-star staff such as brigadiers were almost the office juniors. They often came to the Ministry having commanded a fighting brigade of three thousand men where they had "god-like" status. They had to come down to a new lowly level in the Ministry of Defence main building, sharing an office with two others and having to make the tea. I knew Pardue from Germany and was happy to chat over tea in my office. I wondered if the approach was connected to the aide's question, so was guarded.

Pardue prefaced the conversation by saying that he was genuinely seeking help for a friend. I laughed and encouraged him to go on. Pardue proceeded to explain that his friend was now a very senior army officer who had risen through the ranks, like a knife through butter, because he was quite brilliant. When the "friend" was a mere colonel some years earlier, he had had a "wobble" in his marriage. Pardue was at pains to point out that the said friend and his wife got over the blip and are now inseparable. She was the "wind beneath his wings" and would be essential in supporting him in his new role. I liked Pardue's style in drawing out the suspense and I added to it by taking Pardue's cup and offering to organise a refill of coffee.

On my return, Pardue was rotating the globe on my

bureau. 'This is beautiful. Germany is one country,' stated Pardue.

I explained to Pardue that it meant I could date the globe to before the Second World War. He seemed interested in the dating of globes, so I asked him if he was a gambling man. I told him that there is a country on the globe he was turning which he would never have heard of as it only existed for twenty years.

Pardue scoffed and told me that he had a passion for maps and it was highly unlikely he would not know a country.

I offered a wager, but Pardue declined.

He guessed correctly that I had made money from this knowledge in the past, so thought better of it. I showed him the red area of Tuva Tannu, a republic that existed from 1921 to 1944 within the Soviet Union.

I explained to a somewhat chastened Pardue that this helped date the globe and probably made it quite valuable. I then said, 'And about your happily married friend?'

Pardue explained that the wife had followed her husband round the world supporting his career. Whilst she had no formal training, she had worked as a secretary, finding this the easiest way of gaining employment and keeping herself sane in the various postings. One of the wife's most important jobs had been in Bielefeld in West Germany, where she worked in the Corps Headquarters. It was during this time that they had their marital wobble. There was a misunderstanding, and the wife thought her husband had "strayed" whilst on a language course at the school of languages. I did think this was a little specific and Pardue was quick to point out it was some years ago, so the detail of the wobble was of little relevance. What was critical was the wife's response. The wife had not thrown her errant husband out, shredded his clothes, nor left him. She had simply removed highly classified, top secret, documents from a safe. The wife had thought to embarrass her husband. Pardue explained that she had never done anything with them and the theft was never discovered.

I was perplexed and wondered how such secret documents, especially those of a higher security classification than Top Secret, could be removed and never noticed. I was so well aware of the security in the Ministry and I had also experienced it in Potsdam. My natural question to Pardue was, 'Why are you telling me this?'

Pardue replied that the friend wanted to return the documents but realised that just "dropping them in" would cause a firestorm, not only for "the friend and his wife", but also for the chain of command in Bielefeld and the reputational damage to the army.

I then suggested that the documents could simply be shredded or burned.

Pardue said that this had been the first suggestion. 'Unfortunately, the total number of documents that were missing,' he then checked himself, and said, 'They are not documents, but eight-inch floppy discs – are recorded.' He explained, 'They were then the new storage medium and may not have been as well looked after in the headquarters as the more conventional paper secret files.' So, whilst the information was probably secure, the physical discs were the problem.

The Second Division forward headquarters would be returning to York and would be subject to a rigorous pre-move security audit. It isn't inconceivable that a sharp security officer would notice that two empty discs were missing. Furthermore, the higher command, to whom it had been fully disclosed, believe that the discs should be recovered and returned to the headquarters. Pardue pointed out that the headquarters was still in Bielefeld and so, although slim, there was still an international threat. Thankfully, the documents were some years old and the relevance to a foreign power would be limited.

Pardue said, 'This is an arse-wiping exercise. We are

trying to clean up someone's mess.'

I asked why was I being involved and was this not a uniform rather than a suit issue?

Pardue's response made me grin. 'When it comes to arse-wiping, the suits are best with the paperwork'.

I asked if there was a timeframe and was told that as the friend was to take up a senior appointment on 10th April, it would be helpful if everything was sorted by then.

I said I would think about whether I could help.

'If you are able to assist, you would get a big pat on the back from the Minister,' Pardue explained.

'Pat on the back? Spare me, that is usually reconnaissance for a dagger,' I responded.

Pardue laughed, spun the globe as he left and said, 'Tuva!'

It didn't take long for me to work out who was being appointed and into which role on 10th April and why this revelation was so sensitive. I could even identify the wife and thought that Jocasta and I may have even met her. I wasn't sure why the solution needed to be so sophisticated, but it did allow my creative juices to flow. A dead letter box in Pall Mall, a tryst at the burlesque club, swapping briefcases in Hyde Park. I was sure John le Carre never had to come up with an absurd plot to recover obsolete documents as a favour for a friend. I called it Operation Tuva.

## Attachment 24

## Common Sense

*Politicians, journalists, business and religious leaders usually cry for "common sense" or a "common sense" approach whenever there is a problem. Common sense is seldom common and very often makes no sense. Aristotle set the hare running several millennia ago when he talked of the "golden mean" which many people associated with "being reasonable" and using "common sense", but this is mistaken. There is no call for moderation, but an understanding of a position that is based upon reason. For example, the virtue between cowardice and foolhardiness is courage. Courage is not defined by running away when scared, which may seem reasonable, but neither is it mounting a futile attack. Courage depends on reason and often means acting against one's best interest and common sense.*

*In July 1916, during the Battle of the Somme, Private James Millar was ordered to take a message under heavy artillery fire over open ground and return with an answer. On leaving the trench, he was shot through his back with the bullet exiting through his abdomen. Holding a dressing to his wound, he delivered the message and returned with the reply before falling dead. Private Millar was to receive one of 638 Victoria Crosses awarded during the First World War for acts of conspicuous bravery. No one would have blamed Private Millar had he used his common sense and declined to continue with his mission. Common sense is often an excuse to take the easy option or do nothing.*

## A P Stein

I had a problem and I decided that it did not need common sense, it needed a dose of theatre and I knew just the actor!

My first problem was the collection of the "documents" from the outskirts of Warminster. The house was less than ten miles from my own. I was advised that the documents fitted snuggly in a tennis racket cover. I made my first mistake in assuming that matters of this nature were easy. I rang a surprised Jocasta and asked her to collect the tennis racket from a friend as I intended to take up tennis. In all the years Jocasta had known me, she had never seen me play any sport, show any inclination to play or watch or discuss sport, so she was seriously confused.

Jocasta was also surprised that I had friends in the area. I explained that I wanted to have something I could play with the twins and tennis seemed sensible. Jocasta suggested I simply go out and buy a new racket. Why would I need a gift of an old racket? I agreed and told her not to bother. I was unsettled, as it meant I would have to go and collect the racket myself, as I had no-one I could take into my confidence or trusted in Wiltshire. By bringing Jocasta into the equation, I had created a situation where I could not just turn up with the original racket, I would have to buy a new racket. I asked a colleague where was the best place to buy one and he directed me to Lillywhites in Piccadilly. Even this simple task is fraught with bear traps if you are as disinterested in sport as I was. I had presumed that I would go into the sports shop and buy a racket. I had no idea that there were racks and racks to choose from in every material and colour. In the event, I simply bought the one with the most discreet cover.

I seldom drove in Frome, as Jocasta had a car and I did not need a car in London. So whilst Warminster was less than ten miles from Frome, it seemed a rather difficult place to get to. In the end, I simply headed from Lillywhites and took the Thursday afternoon train from Waterloo that I would have taken home, but I changed in Salisbury and alighted in Warminster. I took a taxi via the military officer's house and picked up the old tennis racket. I did not speak to the lady of the house, but simply smiled. She avoided my gaze and nodded her head in response, as I thanked her in a stage whisper for the loan. The taxi then took me to Frome Station, where I waited twenty minutes for Jocasta to collect me. The old racket had a small wooden head covered by canvas. When I got back into the taxi, I removed the brown paper containing what seemed to be old computer discs from the canvas cover and put them into the new racket cover. They easily fitted in the new cover which had a huge head.

When the taxi dropped me off at the station, I had one last check in the old racket cover to make sure it was empty, and I then tried to put it with the old racket in a waste bin. It stuck out too far and looked odd, so I pushed it under a metal railing into bushes whilst bending to look as if I was fastening my shoelace. I did feel ridiculous, but no one seemed to notice.

Jocasta was so impressed by my smart new racket when she arrived at the station to pick me up, that she wanted to look at it immediately. I put her off by saying it could wait until we were home. She said she was inspired to join me and try tennis with the twins. We would make up a foursome. When we got out of the car, Jocasta wanted to see the racket. Luckily, I was able to hand it to her as I removed it from the cover whilst leaving the discs still inside. It reminded me to be careful. I was anxious to transfer them to my briefcase and get them back to London. On the Saturday, Jocasta pointed out to me that before we could all play tennis, I needed shoes, socks, shorts, shirts, balls and a court. I was relieved that despite my new racket, tennis was to remain aspirational for the family at least on the first weekend.

Back in London, I settled into a work routine, content that the discs were secure in my safe at my flat.

## Attachment 25

## North East Man

*It is uncanny that scientists know how much testosterone you were exposed to in the womb by the ratio of length of your index finger with your ring finger. What if other aspects of your hand were based on scientific fact? As you gaze at your palm, what if the "life" line did give specific details of your life and your "heart" line gave details of your love? Students would flock to graduate in palmistry. Parents could plan their new baby's christening and at the same time book the wedding and the funeral. The real skill, however, would be understanding the success and wealth lines. Would you disclose your inadequate success line on your CV? Would you let a girlfriend see your dodgy wealth line? Would that dreadful date be made all the more attractive if he had a wonderful wealth line and a very short lifeline?*

**Gordon Shawcross**

Caroline and I left Putney at 11 o'clock in the morning. We did skip to the Putney Bridge Tube. I had never skipped before and it never occurred to me just how tiring it was. We were both still laughing at what people must have thought; then I paused. I had had a good idea and I needed a rest. Why didn't we just go back to Haston's friend's flat and ask him if he had seen Haston? Caroline had not been aware of the full story so was rather perplexed by my sudden change of demeanour. I explained that whilst we were going to see Geordie and Sheena for lunch, the plan was that we would discuss Haston. Haston being the "orange" man. Caroline was confused; so on the Tube from Putney to Earl's Court, which took seven minutes, I gave her the abbreviated backstory. Caroline had mixed emotions. She felt that the whole situation could be dangerous and kept saying "treason" but she also had the same curiosity as I did. I explained how I had dragged Sheena and Geordie into the plot.

We were not due in Harcourt Terrace until noon, so we wandered through Earl's Court to pick up some small gift for Sheena. We were rather disappointed that all the shops were the same. There were no shops that stood out as individual or unusual. I told Caroline how my one fear was that I was becoming bland and faceless. Just another boring man in insurance. Caroline scolded me in a mocking manner. 'But you have just swept me off my feet and could soon be in prison for treason. How boring is that?!' she exclaimed.

Geordie and Sheena were delighted to see us. Caroline handed over the flowers that we had bought in the absence of a proper gift. Sheena was pleased and put them in a vase whilst Geordie organised drinks. Geordie had never been a drinker. His time behind the record decks had been a window into alcohol abuse. He had seen men and women behave in outrageous ways and he always vowed he would never let alcohol cloud his mind or judgement. Thumper had liked Newcastle Brown Ale and so Geordie always kept a couple of bottles in his fridge as a homage to his heritage. The other strange drink that Geordie and Sheena did enjoy was Harvey's Bristol Cream. This was again a throwback to Thumper who called it "Hardy's Bristol Cream" and considered it to be a posh drink that he and Geordie should drink on a Sunday before lunch.

Caroline, Geordie and Sheena and I sat down to enjoy the sherry. I explained that I had told Caroline the full Haston story and that I had had an idea. I would go back to Embankment Gardens and simply ask "Humphrey" if he knew where Haston was.

Geordie was less enthusiastic and felt it would be better to ring Lela and find out where his flat was near Madam YoJo's.

Caroline cut across both of us and said, 'Surely it is time for us all to find a decent, or maybe indecent, burlesque show?' There were high fives all round and Geordie was dispatched to his favourite newsagents to buy *Time Out*. Being Geordie, he sensibly came back with four copies so we could work in parallel, rather than series.

After what Sheena called a "North East man" roast

lunch prepared by Sheena, with some help from Caroline, Sheena and Caroline washed up. Geordie and I did offer to help, but Sheena declined, announcing that she was happy to play the stereotype for the benefit of Caroline, as we had only just met and she wanted to demonstrate domestic harmony. I pointed out that I had known Caroline since she was a girl. She was my childhood sweetheart.

It is surprising just how many cabaret and burlesque theatres exist in London, but we picked three that seemed to be the most promising. Of the three, the Belle Époque and the Bohemian burlesque show were within walking distance of each other, and we decided to go to both.

## Attachment 26

## Solutions

*When NASA was trying to put men on the moon, their greatest problem was trying to find a metal module strong enough to withstand the heat of re-entry. They continually failed. Some bright spark then changed the problem. The problem, he suggested, was not how to protect the module but how to protect the men that were inside it. NASA came up with the ablative heatshield. The shield did not withstand heat, it simply burnt away. NASA changed the problem and then solved it.*

**Ryan Haston**

Quentin was buzzing with excitement and could not wait to tell me of the new plans, new show and new beginnings. Quentin was waving papers and summoned over Gino and Steve. He ushered us all into Steve's office, which was always where they met, as it was the cleanest. Quentin was surprised to see me in so early but believed it was fate because he wanted to involve me in the plans. The owner, pleased with the growing popularity of the theatre, had agreed to Quentin's plan for a makeover. The venue would be repainted, the furniture renewed, the bar repositioned and we would open with Quentin's new show. The theatre would close for almost two weeks on the 29th March and reopen on 10th April.

All of the work was to be completed before the end of the tax year. I did see where the owner's self-interest may have crept in there. Steve was somewhat cynical because he had not been consulted.

But Quentin said, 'Oh, but you had. Remember your layout and drawings for the perfect theatre competition?'

Steve said, 'Yes, but that was years ago.'

Quentin replied, 'But I kept the copy that you threw in the skip. I added Gino's suggestions for the bar that he gave you when you interviewed him for job of bar manager. We just needed my new show and a star...' Quentin then gestured to me.

Quentin was not good at responding to the barrage of questions, he was a big hand, small map sort of leader. It was Steve who stepped up and took control. He began with a list of everyone's questions and worked methodically through what would need to happen. He drew up a schedule of meetings and agreed to meet the owner with Quentin. I was told by Steve that every year they were promised a makeover and every year it had been withdrawn. Quentin said that this year would be different, they were making money. I had not seen Quentin so animated, so I felt at least Quentin was convinced it would happen.

Quentin had fleshed out *The Shaming of the Few*. He pointed out that the film *Cabaret* dealt with fascism, race and politics. His new show would deal with equality, gender and discrimination. It would go back to the burlesque roots and deal in mockery. I was not won over, but trusted Quentin's instinct. I did ask if the owner had any artistic influence and was assured they were indifferent to what went on. I felt that the stars were all starting to align. I would use the two weeks break to get my life in order. I had found stability and contentment.

Stein and I had arranged to set aside Monday evening to watch *Oklahoma!*. We had both been so busy that we had not had a period to relax. Stein had been up and down to Frome.

Before *the bright golden haze* hit *the meadow* and *the corn was as high as an elephant's eye*, Stein asked me if I would do him a favour. He needed a parcel taken to Germany and it was rather sensitive and, if I was willing, he would be very grateful. He told me that he had looked at the train timetables and I could be there and back in two days. I was secretly thrilled.

I told Stein that I would love to go, as I potentially had a week off whilst the theatre was being revamped and I was at a loss to know what to do. I had thought of going to York, as I had spent six years there and it was my favourite city. I wanted Stein to go with me at some time so I could show him the Minster.

Stein reminded me that he had spent every year till he went up to Oxford in Durham and knew the Minster and it was not a patch on Durham Cathedral. We laughed when we realised how we were playing one-upmanship with churches. Stein mentioned St Nicholas and Leipzig and much of the rest of the night was spent on churches. Stein told me that he wished Jocasta could be a fly on the wall listening to him wax lyrical about churches. It was agreed I would have to visit Frome to meet her and the children.

I was not free until the following Wednesday to go to Germany, but was happy to help. Stein said he would get everything organised.

*Oklahoma!* had been brilliant, and Stein and I agreed that we would watch all the Rodgers and Hammerstein back catalogue over the coming months. Stein could not believe how his musical taste had developed from Mendelssohn. He wanted to introduce me to Gilbert and Sullivan but said that maybe that could wait.

I was leaving the club late on the Thursday evening following the Monday *Oklahoma!* session, when I was taken by the arm. It was Robert. 'Mr Cross,' he said, 'Please can we drive you home?' We both climbed into the back of a black Mercedes. It was almost a limousine, since the driver seemed so far from me as I sat back in my plush seat. Robert asked how I was enjoying the job and I conceded that it was marvellous.

I was quizzed as to my accommodation.

I replied that it was very comfortable and I was living

with Stein. Robert indicated that he was aware and pressed me as to whether I was sharing a bed with Stein.

I do not know why, but I felt affronted and angry. Stein was my friend and I found myself feeling protective towards him. I replied, 'No!' quite emphatically.

Robert said, 'Me thinks the lady do protest too much.' I thought back to how blind Robert was to Shakespeare back in Estonia and here he was trotting it out. I kept my counsel.

Robert questioned me about Stein's friends and routines and I could not really help, as I had never met any of his friends and never knew of his routines. Robert was irritable and asked me why I was being so difficult. This annoyed me even more. I turned in my seat so I could look directly at Robert.

I asked, 'What was my task? What was I to find out? What instructions have I?' In my interrogation of Robert, I also found myself asking, 'And who are you and who is your organisation?'

Robert was uncomfortable and started adjusting his glasses which I had seen him do when he was nervous. He softened and in a patronising way told me I was doing a terrific job and everyone was pleased with me.

I was not giving up and wanted to know who everyone was.

Robert told me I would get the "full gen" tomorrow and said I would meet everyone when this matter was sorted. I was less than convinced.

The rest of the journey was quiet until, like an idiot, I raised the fact that I was off to Germany. I bit my lip so hard after I said it that I could taste blood. I went into a sweat and could not understand why I had mentioned it. Robert did not need to know. The cat was out of the bag and I now could not recover from the full explanation. I could not say why I was going to Germany, nor what I was to take with me as I had not been told, but I had raised Robert's level of awareness. Robert was very interested in knowing more but I was reluctant to say anything further. I was dropped off in Flood Street further from the flat than I hoped.

Robert said, 'We will be in touch.'

As I stepped out of the car, I paused and asked Robert, 'Oh and by the way, what happened to Marta?' It may have been the street light, but I was sure that Robert's face went pale.

Robert fiddled with his glasses and mumbled something. I thought it was, 'Who?'

So I said, 'The ballerina.'

Robert scoffed and waved his hand. 'Ballet school, of course,' and he signalled the driver to leave.

I was troubled by Robert's reply, as I now knew Marta was back in the USSR. It was inconceivable that the girl referred to from Neeme in Stein's *Radio Times* report was not the same girl I had driven to the troupe. *Back in the USSR*, the Beatles' song, became a worm in my head which I couldn't shake off, even when I was home and lying in my bed.

Next morning, I was a man on a mission. I would normally spend most of the morning in bed, then eventually rise to do my personal administration. This could be shopping or washing and ironing. I would finish in the early afternoon for a quiet time reading and then towards evening head to the West End. This morning, I was up and out and in the West End by eleven. I found Lela asleep on her sofa. She pretended to be angry with me, but after I had given her a large overpayment for the rent arrears, she was back as my best friend. I asked if I could collect my bike and some effects and she told me they were where I had left them.

I could not carry all my clothes, which were still in a large box, but I could collect my smaller administration box and precious Brompton bike, which, despite being jammed behind the freezer in what was effectively an outhouse, was in perfect order. I opened it up, still as pleased with the mechanism now as I was when I bought it some two years earlier. I had not actually bought it as such but had lent some money to a friend who was helping to launch a bike shop. Whilst the money was lost along with the friendship, I managed to retain the bike. I had to fashion a strap from a couple of ties to secure the box, but it worked and I was able to cycle back to Chelsea. I was anxious to find my papers regarding the Shakespeare Touring Company and particularly my payslips. I thought I had been a fool. I had somehow assumed Robert was on my side, but I now had no idea which side was which. I had carried out all my tasks in Estonia without once questioning what Robert was up to. I felt sick and sweaty as I cycled home and it was from a growing anxiety that I may have called all of this wrong.

I folded my bike and took it with my box into Stein's flat. I rifled through the box and found the offer letter from the Touring Shakespeare Company. It had been addressed to my student flat in Hammersmith, but I remembered it had been handed to me on my last admin day at LAMDA. My only surprise when I was given it was that I needed no audition and the tour was some six months in the future. The letter had been signed by Robert Harold, Tour Manager. I found my pay statements, I was paid, in sterling, monthly during the tour into my Yorkshire Bank Account. The payment came from the TSC. Save for now recalling Robert's full name, I had learnt nothing new.

I went to the theatre early and found Steve, the manager, as I expected. Steve spent much of the day in the theatre and usually left halfway through the evening show. He said he was "tickets, tables and toilets" and did not need to be involved in the "show stuff". He left that to Quentin. I was fêted by Steve on arrival, as I was the new attraction. I used the bonhomie to ask Steve how I was selected for the role at the Bohemian. Steve was perplexed and said, 'You were recommended, weren't you?'

'Yes,' I answered, 'but by whom?'

Steve went back to his office. He had a seriously tidy office and was obsessional about hygiene. Gino had told me that Steve had once had a drug problem, which he was over, but that the addictive behaviour remained. Steve went directly to his locked filing cabinet and the staff folders. He went straight to A-C and picked out Cross. It was empty.

'Oh! That isn't right.' Steve pondered.

I asked if anyone would have a key or need access and Steve said, 'No'.

I did not want to make it an issue so laughed it off. Steve tried to, as well, but I could tell he was not content.

Steve told me that he would find the contents, as they must have been misfiled. I knew from Steve's face that they would not have been.

I was beginning to think that I was in too deep. Stein seemed a genuine friend. There may be ten or so years between us, but we were equals. I was weighing up the two conflicting sides to the equation and it was Robert's side that troubled me. I could not put my finger on it, except that Stein had always been open and honest with me and had no reason to be; whilst Robert was not and had no reason not to be. It was going round in my head, but I was suitably distracted when Quentin came over.

Whilst I did have a new show to learn, I knew it would not take my whole ten-day break. I was minded delaying the trip to Bielefeld and maybe make it a long weekend so I could see some other parts of Germany. I also wanted to spend some time getting myself organised and make a life outside work. It occurred to me that I should make contact with Geordie again. I had only been to one Trust Meeting and had liked him and his girlfriend. I was surprised that the school had chosen Geordie as the other trustee, but guessed that as he lived in London and the trust was in London, he was the natural choice. I also wondered who Edward Hardy was. Mark had said the trust had almost half a million pounds bequeathed, so I presumed he was a rich old boy. I was also mindful that he might be interested in other art or theatre-based investments. I was not even sure if Edward Hardy was alive and I was annoyed with myself that I had not asked more questions at the meeting. I was disorganised. I had been trying to renew my driving licence but as I did not have a permanent address, this was proving difficult. I had thought of using the Bohemian or even the flat above Madam YoJo's, but even they were subject to change. It was whilst musing over my address and lifestyle that I had another thought. *Who was paying for the flat above Madam YoJo's?* I had taken my kitbag from there and so had effectively moved out, but I could go back and try to find out. I could tell anyone who asked that I was picking up my mail and was leaving my key. In any event, Robert had arranged it in the first place, so presumably I was still in occupation, as far as Robert's people knew.

That night after the show, I went back to the flat. I had meant to drop my key off anyway when I first left, but decided to wait to see how life worked out in Embankment Gardens. I was pleased my key still worked. The flat smelt musty and I had forgotten just how scruffy it was. There were three men living there, all were working in theatres. One was security as he had a lanyard that always hung by the front door, presumably so he did not forget it. The name on the lanyard was James Bull. I was curious that it was always hanging there even when James Bull was out, so either he did not use it or he always forgot to take it. The second man, who I had met, was in a chorus. He had moved in just before me to replace my original roommate.

No one was home, albeit it was one thirty in the morning. I did wonder whether they worked for Robert too. I was not sure what I was looking for, but thought a utility bill or letter may disclose the landlord. Like all accommodation of this nature, there was a bundle of unopened post and unsolicited mail stacked up by the door for previous tenants, many of whom, like me, craved a permanent home for their mail. I gave a cursory look round before taking the bundle of post and cycling home. It only took 25 minutes to cycle from the theatre to Stein's front door. I would normally shower and then be in bed by one. Tonight, I was running late, but was still able to get a good night's sleep and be up at nine, having almost seven hours sleep.

Stein was having coffee when I surfaced. He had noted the bundle of post and asked me what was happening.

I explained that I had called in at my old flat and did not have time to sort the post as it was late and dark. I asked Stein how long he was going to be at the flat as I needed to chat.

Stein told me to grab a coffee and I could have his undivided attention. I made two coffees in the cafetière and whilst it took longer, it gave me time to set the scene. I poured the coffee and we both sat down on the sofa.

I first tentatively asked whether I had done something wrong by reading the reports wrapped in the *Radio Times* folder.

Stein said that if they were secret, he would not have left them out and whilst they were sensitive, he could quite see why I would find them interesting. Stein told me he kept them as a reminder of what had happened during his current appointment.

I asked if I could show one of those reports to Stein that was causing me trouble. Stein picked up the folder and gave it to me, so I went straight to the report on the deporting of Marta. I explained that the name was redacted but the home town and timings seemed too much of a coincidence. I then went on to explain the minor role I played in Marta's trip from Estonia to London. There was a long pause before Stein responded.

'Absence of the normal, presence of the abnormal,' grinned Stein. 'Let me check on the name and we can see if there is anything sinister in this,' he added. Stein told me he was pleased that I had broached the subject, but I was not expecting his next question, which was, 'Do you have anything else you want to tell me?'

I flustered that I did not, but I knew from Stein's wry grin that he was not convinced. I was annoyed, as it was always the same in auditions. All my prepared work was great, but I would be thrown off by the "and one more thing" request.

Stein went through to the kitchen to tidy up the coffee cups and I went through the post and was able to discard all but one letter. It was for the attention of Mr R Harold. It was from the Westminster City Council, acknowledging the payments of rates. I was desperate to show Stein, but decided to wait to see if the Marta link showed up anything of concern. I was minded that the letter was a further link to Robert that would cause Stein to probe further.

Stein came back into the lounge and asked if I had found what I was looking for.

I said no and waffled on about needing a driving licence. Stein had a brown square envelope.

Stein went on to say, 'This is the parcel for Bielefeld and these are your first-class tickets by train.' He added that the ferry is Dover to Calais and that I would have to change trains a couple of times before I got to Dusseldorf. All the tickets were flexible, save that if I missed the Dusseldorf connection, it may be sensible for me to take a taxi. Stein told me that he had changed the code on the safe so only he and I would know what it was. I looked at the piece of paper on which Stein had written the new code. It was my profession to learn lines and I had a marvellous memory; except for numbers. I put the note in my pocket. Stein told me that he would be away with Jocasta and the girls in Ireland whilst I was away. He trusted me to deliver the package to a Captain Jacobs, who would meet me at the guard room to the entrance to Catterick Barracks. Stein told me that he was simply tidying up a historical military mistake and it was not a ministry matter, which was why he was grateful for my help.

My loyalties were being torn. It was increasingly clear that Stein trusted me with the safe code. The package could not be too sinister if it was being handed to a British military officer at a British military base. I was coming to the conclusion that Robert was the problem.

My problem reappeared the following night. Same hand on my elbow, but this time I had my bike, so it had to be folded down before we could take the same walk to the Mercedes. Unlike the previous occasion, we stopped the car on the embankment at the rear of the MOD main building. Robert was aware that I was anxious and started reassuring me that everything was fine. Robert pointed to the building and explained to me what it was and how important it was to the defence of the realm. Robert explained that whilst Stein had been working in East Germany, he had been blackmailed by a young girl who was working for the Stasi. Robert went on to say that Stein's behaviour had changed, and whilst he was once quiet and reserved, he was now what Robert called "a party animal". Naturally, the government wanted to watch him and know what he was up to. Robert seemed earnest when he reassured me that Stein was being considered for the top job in the Ministry, but that they could not sanction it unless he was squeaky clean. Stein had to be Caesar's wife, beyond reproach. Robert wanted me to know that they wished Stein absolutely no ill will, they simply wished to fully understand him.

'And if he is working for the Soviets?' I asked.

Robert answered that if that was the case, it was better

they knew sooner rather than later, for all concerned.

Robert wanted to know the full details of my planned trip to Germany. Was I going to East or West Germany? And why Stein was using me and not any number of conventional or indeed unconventional military couriers?

I confessed that I had no idea, except that Stein had told me it was not an MOD issue. Robert seemed to think this confirmed his story and that it should satisfy me that I needed to trust him. It did, to a certain extent. Robert had not fiddled with his glasses once and I was swinging back to think he was the good guy and was wearing the white hat.

I explained to Robert that if I simply gave the documents to him, I would lose Stein's trust and Stein would know he was exposed. Robert countered my objection, which he agreed was valid, with a simple solution. After I had taken the parcel from the safe on the designated day, I would be picked up by his people. They would examine the content and return it to me so I could continue with the parcel to Germany. Stein would be none the wiser.

Reassured, I found myself agreeing to the plan. Robert asked when I was due to go to Germany.

On impulse, I said Saturday 1st April, in the morning, even though I was hoping to go later. Robert was happy to run with the date and dropped me off. He told me that we would be meeting again and that I should, in the meantime, try and fill in all the gaps regarding the trip, not least where exactly in Germany I was going and with whom I was to meet.

Robert's reassurance waned, the longer I had time to think. I was seriously troubled; I needed someone I trusted to talk to. I could think of no-one, and it made me realise just how shallow and friendless I was. In desperation, I rang Geordie, but Geordie was not in; he was up north. It was Sheena who answered and recognised my voice.

Sheena asked if she could help; I found myself asking Sheena if I could use their address for my mail to be delivered. I had wanted to have a safe place to have my driving licence delivered and so it seemed like a sensible excuse for the call. Sheena gave me an address in Albert Mansions that Geordie still owned. She said I could use the address and where I could pick up mail.

I was very grateful and I told Sheena I would speak soon.

I was losing sleep. Stein had gone to what he called his "beach hut in Bray" with Jocasta and the children for half term or something. I had the flat to myself, but that made me even more nervous. I was sure I had been followed to work, and I was becoming increasingly paranoid. I wondered if I should go to ground for a couple of days to avoid the next assignation with Robert, or more worrying, Robert's people. I could still go on the Saturday. I could go to Bielefeld without the package being compromised. Robert would get other chances to expose Stein, if Stein was a villain, but they could do so without my help. This plan did seem the most sensible and the more I thought about it, the better it seemed. All I had to do was stay low from the Thursday until the following Wednesday. It would mean missing two nights at the theatre. This plan replaced *Back in the USSR* as the worm in my head.

Quentin quite understood the situation when I approached him. I told him that Mother had had a stroke. Quentin was concerned and of course agreed I must go up north; yes, he would miss me; it was never a good time to lose his leading man but he understood and with the show due to close for two weeks anyway, etc, etc. I was careful never to lie to Quentin, maybe just slightly mislead him. My late mother had died of a stroke, albeit some decade earlier and I was going north, but to North Germany.

After the show on the Wednesday night, I left through the fire door by the back of the stage. I had positioned my bike beside the door already assembled. I returned to Chelsea via Trafalgar Square. It was a slightly longer route, but I wanted to vary everything I did. I had no reason to believe I was in any danger; I had no fear of Robert, but I just felt vulnerable and used. I so wanted to get all this over. I had never had any self-doubt, nor feelings of inadequacy in my whole life, but the situation had started to control me.

At the bottom of Tite Street, I saw a black Mercedes and whilst in that part of London most cars were Mercedes, I ducked into Dilke Street. I folded my bike and went to investigate on foot. There was definitely someone waiting in a car as the internal light was on. I checked my watch. Strangely, the Rolex gave me some comfort. It was giving me a superpower. It made me concentrate and feel strong. If they had left the club, say ten minutes after discovering that I had gone, they would be waiting for me to arrive about now. The bottom of Tite Street joined Chelsea Embankment and gave the occupants of the Mercedes unhindered views of all access and egress from the flat. I had no idea what to do, so I cycled to the Chelsea Embankment Gardens and rested on a bench, using my Brompton wheel as a pillow. It was surprisingly comfortable. I must have been tired, as I dropped off to sleep. I awoke a couple of times during the night and toyed with riding home, but I felt the cold evening was my punishment and I was being tested in my resolve. At sunrise, I told myself that I had passed the test. I felt quite sprightly. I unfolded my bike and cycled to the end of Dilke Street. There was no Mercedes, so I took a chance on a quick ride to the flat, watching for any sign of life. I had prepacked my old kit bag with a change of clothing for Bielefeld. I just grabbed it and left. I had no idea where to head, but I knew I wanted to be clear of the flat until Saturday had passed.

Thursday went quite quickly. I went to the National Portrait Gallery. I knew I would need to head back to Victoria before the Saturday, but I would be miles from trouble in the meantime. The National Portrait Gallery were bike tolerant, but they did not like my kitbag. I had to use some charm with the girl on the cloakroom duty. I suggested that the kitbag was my puncture repair kit and she relented. I had forgotten my washbag, otherwise I would have used the toilets for a wash and shave. When cursing myself for forgetting the wash bag I realised I had also forgotten the package to go to Bielefeld. I would have cried had I not been able to laugh. I was so disorganised in my head and in my life. I told myself that when this farce was all over, I would get my life back in some sort of order. I now had to risk returning to the flat. It was a stupid error and I kept reproaching myself. I was making lists in my head of places I could hide and people I could seek help from, but my heart rate was rising, and I was feeling hot and bothered. I sat down on a central bench between two art students sketching from the same portrait and put my head in my hands.

Nell Gwyn came to my rescue. The large Simon Verelst painting that was being copied by the art students was looking down on me. Nell Gwyn was smiling at me and the students. I wandered over to read the citation.

Eleanor Gwyn, or "Pretty, witty Nell", as Pepys called her, came to London as an orange-seller, rose to become one of the leading comic actresses of the day, and mistress to the King, Charles II. The playwright Dryden supplied her with a series of saucy, bustling parts, ideally suited to her talents.

I thought to myself, *Jaffa, you too can become the leading actor of the day. Quentin will write the parts, ideally suitable for my talents.* This cheered me up no end, and in a brighter disposition, I started to think clearly. I sat back down between the girls and expressed my envy at their talent, as they had both captured their profiles of Nell so well. They both thanked me but then put away their equipment and left me alone feeling slightly guilty that perhaps I had driven them off. I blew a kiss to Nell and mouthed, 'Thank you.'

What were my options? I need not go to Bielefeld, but I would be letting down Stein. I could fall in with Robert's plan and that would also let Stein down. I could send someone else with the package. This idea had merit. I could send a motorcycle courier. It would involve others and I would lose control. I was thinking so much better under the watchful eye of Nell. I could go to Germany but have Robert pick up someone else with a package. I had any number of actor friends, or rather, acquaintances. They could play "Cross" and on Saturday morning take an alternative package to Robert. I mulled over the complexity in all of the plans. It did seem that any plan had to be simple to work, and any of the plans needing help would mean placing my trust in someone. I did not know anyone I could trust; maybe Steve or Quentin. I had burnt my boats with Quentin, as he thought I was up North and Steve was out of the question, as it was he that organised my job at the Bohemian. I gazed at pretty, witty Nell and it hit me. Shawcross! Shawcross would be perfect. I could get Shawcross's address from the school. Geordie said he lived in London.

I headed straight to the three phone boxes in a row on Charing Cross Road. I would collect my bike later. I had no idea whether the school would be open, as Stein had mentioned that it was half term, but I pressed on. I rang directory enquiries and was given the school number and then rang the school. I told the Old Boys' Association secretary, Mrs Alexander, that I had invitations to send out for my 30th birthday and could not find Gordon Shawcross's address. I was delighted with the ease that Shawcross's address was obtained. I used the opportunity to give Mrs Alexander my new permanent address as Geordie's flat. I was not sure why, but it seemed to add some credibility to my call.

I would head to Streatham. It was the Thursday evening. I did not want to spend too long with Shawcross to give him time to think. This needed some blind obedience from Shawcross and some fine acting from me. I redeemed my bike and kitbag from the cloakroom. It was almost a crisis as I handed over the piece of paper with the code to the safe rather than the cloakroom ticket, but thankfully, the helpful girl noticed.

She asked if it was my phone number and if it was, she was happy to phone me.

Her smile was so wide, and her eyes sparkled so much that I said, 'I am off to Germany today, but when I come back, it will be to see both Nell Gwyn and the beautiful girl at the National Portrait Gallery.'

My spirits were uplifted and I think the girl's were too, as she squealed.

I had to struggle across London again. This time, I headed over Waterloo Bridge and south of the river. I ate in an Indian restaurant off Brixton Road. My only company was my bike, as I wanted to keep an eye on it. I was desperate for a wash and shave, but resisted the temptation. I decided to spend the Thursday night in Brockwell Park and then spend Friday at the Dulwich Gallery. I wanted to arrive with Shawcross looking like I really needed help. It was going to be some method acting, I was swinging between thinking I was a fool and thinking I was being followed. On several occasions I had to pause, wiggle my toes and moderate my breathing just like I had been taught at drama school when trying to calm my nerves.

Brockwell Park closed at 10 o'clock so I slipped in and hid behind some trees. It felt safer to be locked in, albeit I was not alone. I was approached by a couple of the local park dwellers wanting alcohol, fags or something stronger. They were quite menacing until I stood up to my full height and they both thought better of arguing with me. I was no fighter, and it made me anxious. I did not sleep, but it all added to my method acting. I was going to have to be in role by that evening. Unsurprisingly, Dulwich Gallery did not want a kitbag, did not want a bike and certainly didn't want me. I was quite pleased to be asked to leave as it meant I had created the correct image. It did occur to me that Shawcross may not even be in; but I thought Nell Gwyn would not have advised me of the plan if that had been the case.

It is extremely hard to kill eight hours in London if you are unkempt and are part of the great unwashed. I was moved on by shopkeepers every time I stopped near a shop. If everyone who gave me a disapproving look had given me a pound, I would have been rich. My slide into street poverty had taken only forty eight hours. My scariest moment was when I was confronted by a policeman. I almost held my wrists together and said, 'Yes, it is me, I will come quietly,' presuming I was being arrested. My fear was unfounded. The policeman was surprisingly pleasant, he just requested some proof that the Brompton bike belonged to me. Luckily, I had my equity card in my wallet and the constable accepted that I was preparing for a part in a gritty street drama. I realised that I needed to lose the bike as it did not fit well with my new image. I found a bike rack at Streatham Hill station. I had a combination lock and chain that I wove through the folded frame and wheels. I so did not want to leave it, but it was becoming a hindrance.

Shawcross's Streatham house was further from Streatham Hill station than the names would suggest. When I finally got there, no one answered the door; it was 9 o'clock at night. I went back to Streatham High Road and looked for somewhere to sit where I could watch. I had only been sleeping rough for two nights and yet I had the smell or look of failure. Even the kebab shop was reluctant to serve me and that seemed to be filled with unsavoury characters. I realised that I was a snob and I wanted to return to a better life once this ordeal was over. I was shocked that I thought it was an "ordeal", as it was such a self-inflicted situation and I could extract myself at any time. I pondered over the plight of all those homeless people that I would step over as they lay in the theatre doorway. I made myself a promise that I would never be disrespectful to them again. I had no sooner had my doner kebab served when I saw a distinctive figure of a man who could be Shawcross walking up Streatham High Road towards me. The chap seemed to be stooped and I thought I was mistaken. I was not, it was Shawcross, and he was kicking a can. I could not believe it, a be-suited businessman kicking a can. I was pleased to see the can being picked up and placed in the bin almost outside the kebab shop. I left before my coffee was brought over and only had a chance to take one bite of the kebab. It was covered in chilli sauce. I grabbed my kitbag and stayed behind Shawcross until we were almost outside Shawcross's flat and then I pounced. Shawcross was startled at first and put up his fists. I wanted to laugh at the posture and shriek that only Shawcross could face a potential mugger by putting up his fists; but I was playing the victim.

I mumbled, 'Thank God I've found you. I need help. I need it badly and I need it now.'

The flat was so warm, the heating on full and even though Shawcross turned it down, by the time he had gone to make a coffee, I had fallen asleep. The two nights on the street had taken their toll.

Thankfully, I was woken by Shawcross. I could hardly speak to him as my mouth was dry and burning from the chilli in the kebab. Even after some water, I was mumbling. I was able to ask him to collect the precious parcel. I was able to tell him about my time at drama school, and I think I put his mind at rest. I did not elaborate on the back story or any other aspect, other than I had fallen out with my flatmate, who I called Humphrey, and simply needed my folder without any fuss. The plan seemed so simple. Shawcross was worried by my struggle to speak, and I may have slightly overplayed my discomfort, but it worked. He told me he did not need any further explanation and that I should go to bed. He would go to the flat first thing in the morning and pick up my folder. I gave him the keys, safe code, and address. He told me he would be back before I woke up.

I thought that if Shawcross was followed, spoken to or

hauled over, he would only have my degree certificate and other mementos with him. He would know absolutely nothing of the situation save that he was helping a friend. I could wait a sensible time after Shawcross had been to the flat to collect the folder and then I could call in and grab the proper parcel, my passport, and the travel tickets. I would be at Dover before Shawcross was back in Streatham. I would apologise to Shawcross when everything had blown over. I was particularly pleased when Shawcross agreed to the plan, because it was to be Shawcross that once again saved my skin.

I was worried that I had overslept, as Shawcross had gone when I woke up. I had used the razor in the bathroom when I had had a shower the night before, so I was feeling fresher, albeit I had slept in my clothes. I wrote a short note for Shawcross and then raced to Streatham Hill station to recover my bike.

I had no idea how far I was behind Shawcross, not least because I had no idea what time he had left and no idea how Shawcross would get to Chelsea. I was pleased that my bike was untouched, and I pedalled off to catch up with, but not overtake, Shawcross. As I approached Albert Bridge, I saw Albert Mansions on my left, the postal address that had been offered by Geordie. I was half tempted to have a closer look, but this was not the time. I went along Dilke Street and looked down Tile Street. There was no Mercedes, and so I ventured down to the Embankment. Luckily, being on my bike meant I was able to quickly turn round when I saw Shawcross in the distance. He was approaching Embankment Gardens from the Chelsea Bridge end. I had beaten him to the flat, so I retreated to Dilke Street to wait. Shawcross would not have expected to see me on a bike, so I felt that whilst we had been close, it was not going to disrupt the plan.

It was Saturday morning and there was very little movement. I had no idea how long to wait. After what appeared to be about half an hour and I was sure that Shawcross had done whatever was necessary, I decided to move. This coincided with a lady coming to her front door to ask me if everything was alright.

I was able to say that I was waiting for my sister, but she must be running late.

I thought sister sounded so much more calming and the lady did too, as she asked me if I needed come in to use her phone.

I thanked her, but declined. I was also minded that being smarter and tidier helped. The day before, she would have called the police.

I had the spare key for the flat. I went in and gathered my own keys off the floor where they had been deposited by Shawcross. I hung the spare on the key press. I went to the safe and tumbled the locks. I usually struggled as I was impatient but, on this occasion, it opened first time. I grabbed the Bielefeld bundle, the train tickets and money but I could not see my passport. After clearing the safe and putting everything back carefully, I could only conclude that Shawcross had been too helpful. *Typical Shawcross*, I thought. I changed my clothes, swapped the kitbag for a small case and placed my bike under my bed. I locked the door on the way out and wondered how I could get out of the country without a passport. Not as easy as you might think, I was to find.

I had to check whether Shawcross had simply done as he was asked. If he had, the folder and passport would be back in Streatham. As I walked to the Tube station in Sloane Square, I thought I had made the wrong decision and that I should have kept my bike with me. It was too late now I was stuck with bus and Tube and the bike would have become an inconvenience, particularly when I headed to Germany. My main concern was that if Robert had picked up Shawcross, he would know that I did not have a passport and he would know that I would head to Streatham. If he had not picked up Shawcross, Shawcross would be heading to Streatham. If truth be told, I had no idea what to do next or where to go. Stein was in Ireland and couldn't be contacted because, given his status, he had to be seriously discreet. He had told me that he would not be safe from the IRA if his position was known. I had the name of the officer in Bielefeld, Captain Jacobs. I wondered if he could be contacted by phone, but this could cause a problem if I had to go through various military exchanges.

I had always relied on charm and luck so, armed only with these qualities, I headed to Waterloo. I was confident that Shawcross would have been intercepted, and I reassured myself that I was taking the best course of action. I stayed overnight in an anonymous bed and breakfast next to Waterloo Station. There was a limited service for the train as it was a Sunday, and I eventually arrived in Dover at 2pm, in perfect time for the 3pm crossing. Perfect if you had the correct travel documentation. My charm was never going to overcome stark bureaucratic procedures. It may have been easy to get Marta into the country, but it was impossible for me to get out. I had learnt from the firm, but helpful, ferry operative that I could get a BVP, a British Visitors Passport, at any main Post Office. Seemingly it only took 20 minutes and cost £12. I was told I needed the usual signed passport photograph and proof of identity. The ferry operative had been particularly keen to help. As he looked at my equity card, he said, 'I am called Cross, I am Simon Cross,' Simon pointed to his name tag.

I tried to pretend we were brothers and so Simon was under an obligation to help, but Simon laughed and pointed to his face.

'This face is from Trinidad,' he grinned, 'so we couldn't have been a very close family.'

It was on the train back to London I realised that proof of ID was my next challenge.

I had applied for a renewal of my driving licence, but this had been delayed, as I had not had a permanent address to send it to. Once Sheena had suggested Albert Mansions, I had had it sent there but I had not collected it. It was also in the name of Haston, as it was a renewal of the driving licence I'd had since I was eighteen and before I even thought of acting and having a stage name. The train journey back to London gave me time to think, although a man next to me was wearing headphones attached to his Walkman, and the white noise that I could hear was becoming more unbearable with every mile we headed to London. Eventually I could take no more and moved seats. I was annoyed with myself for not moving earlier and I reminded myself that most problems could be solved by moving away from the nuisance.

I went into Woolworths beside Victoria Station and found the photobooth. It only took coins and I did not have the correct money. I had to queue at the pick-and-mix to buy some sugary-looking pear drops to get change. This did not go to plan, as I had only grabbed two ounces and so whilst I did get the change, it still was not right for the machine and the shop assistant had already closed the till. Luckily, the lady behind me understood my dilemma even if the shop assistant had not. Armed with the coins, I returned to the booth, only to find that a line of teenagers had been marched there by a teacher to get passport photos for a school trip. I decided to find a café and return later. As I was leaving, the helpful teacher invited me to "push in", as her class would take "forever". I gratefully took up the offer but in my rush to get it over with, I didn't drop the seat far enough and so the photo, when it came out of the slide, had my head too high. By the time I had got to the post office, I had convinced myself that the photos would be rejected and I would need a different set. I collected the passport forms at the post office front counter and was pleased to see that there was a photobooth in the corner.

I was told that I would need proof of my identity and that it could be a passport, driving licence or a shotgun certificate.

When I asked why I would have a passport as ID if I was applying for a passport, the girl became hostile and told me not to be a smart Alec. Any further discussion seemed pointless. I did wish I had the shotgun.

I had hoped my equity card would have been suitable, but it was soundly rejected as the girl was now adamant that I did not have the appropriate evidence. I realised this was all too much for me and I needed a lawyer, so from the kiosk in the post office I rang the only lawyer I knew.

Mark was, as ever, cool and considered. He told me that if I came over to his office in the City, he could certify the photo and provide me with an appropriate comfort letter to attach to a copy of my equity card. It was too late that Monday evening, but Mark was free on the Tuesday at 10.30. I was at a loss to know what to do, so I wandered aimlessly round Victoria until I found a coffee shop where I sat and just watched people.

## Attachment 27

## Adventure

*In the early 18th Century, Mrs Abigail Eischrank of Cambridge, Massachusetts, had thirteen children and whilst large families were quite normal, Abigail could say with absolute certainty that exactly half her children were girls. There is a simple explanation to this fact, but who starts with the simple explanation?*

**Gordon Shawcross**

*Time Out*, the listing magazine essential for anyone wanting to know where to go in London, gave the opening times for the Belle Époque and the Bohemian at half past eight, but we all agreed that we did not want to be too early. Geordie had picked up the three letters addressed to Haston and put them in his pocket for hand delivery. Caroline was on shift at 8 o'clock the next morning and I added that I did not really do late nights. The compromise was that we needed to go early enough to get tickets, if you had to buy them, but not too early to stand out. Geordie was strangely obsessive about punctuality and we all arrived at half past eight and did stand out.

The Belle Époque would have been described by Stein

as risqué. The doormen – and there were three – were huge. They stood too close together when Sheena and Caroline went in and the girls had to almost push them away. Geordie was seething and I stepped forward, asking the girls if everything was alright. The lead bouncer literally looked me up and down. I felt quite threatened, but he growled welcome and made space for all four of us to enter. The place felt sordid. We were ushered to a table by a young girl, who handed out four menus, one to each of us.

Geordie told her we were not eating, but were hoping to meet Sean Cross.

The girl did not understand him, so Sheena repeated what he had said but this too was met by a blank look. Sheena just collected the menus and gave them back. I suggested that I would grab four small drinks from the bar and ask about Haston. If, as I suspected, we were in the wrong place, we could up and leave.

I tried to get a drink at the bar, but the barman explained it was table service.

I asked him about Sean Cross, but he had never heard of him, but then he did not know anyone who worked there as he was new.

We did eventually manage to get four soft drinks from the girl who had dished out the menus. The cabaret was not due to start until nine, and from the flyer on the table, the entertainment was a comedian and judging by the photo, a stripper. I suggested that we leave and head to a local pub to recover. The other three agreed, but only after Caroline had shown mock disappointment at missing the stripper. As we walked briskly from the Belle Époque in no particular direction, Sheena spotted the Bohemian. We had slight reluctance to revisit another seedy joint, but felt compelled, as we were outside.

The Bohemian doorman was dressed in a smart blazer and held the door open for the girls, and I am sure if he had a hat, he would have doffed it to Geordie and I. This time, we had gone in first. We none of us looked like the usual burlesque clientele and a man who looked important came over to introduce himself. This did seem a rather personal touch, but I had only ever been in the Belle Époque, so I had no idea what to expect. The man introduced himself as Quentin, the Show Director. I did feel privileged. Quentin asked us if we had come far and what attracted us to the Bohemian.

It was Sheena who responded explaining that we thought a friend may be in the show and we were going to surprise him. Quentin beamed and ushered us to what he said was the best table.

He asked who the friend was and I stepped in to say Sean, Sean Cross. Quentin was crestfallen. Sean's mother had had a stroke, and he was not performing that night; he had gone up north. Quentin went on to explain that this was the last night before the venue closed for two weeks for refurbishment. Quentin was anxious that we should come back for the grand reopening with his new show, not least because our friend, Sean, was the star. He added that Sean was proving to be popular, as another of his friends had been looking for him the previous night and had been disappointed.

'We might well know him,' said Caroline.

Quentin went quite conspiratorial and whispered, 'Well he has a driver and has picked up Sean several times after work. The doorman says he is called Robert, but I had not met him until last night.'

'He isn't a civil servant, is he?' I asked.

'Oh no, you are thinking of our friend Stein. Stein is on holiday at the moment.' Quentin excused himself, as other guests were coming in and the tables were filling up.

Geordie organised the drinks and Gino brought them over. Gino told the table they were "on the house" and we must all come back for the new show when our friend Sean was back. Gino went on to say this evening's show would not be as good without him, and that he was a great man. Gino's pronunciation and the increasing noise level meant that we all thought that he said Sean was a Greek man. This did cause some confusion and humour when Geordie said, 'No, he is from Middlesbrough.'

Whilst we all enjoyed the show, we were disappointed that we had not found Haston. Geordie was adamant that Haston's parents were long dead and so the idea that he had gone north to see his mother seemed to be a white lie.

I added that from what Quentin said, he was friends with Stein. But we all agreed that without Haston, the evening was a washout. The only new name to have emerged was Robert.

Caroline pointed out that it may have been the fact that Robert was on the scene that caused the fall-out with Stein. We all agreed that there was little more we could do, except open his post. We did so in the taxi home. The letter addressed to R V Haston was a new driving licence, which gave his address at Albert Mansions. This tied in with the reason for the address and confirmed why he had asked Sheena. The other two were from Equity, his trade union, addressed to Mr Cross. One was a monthly circular and the other details of an upcoming election and was in a more formal envelope. We discussed telephoning Lela, but it was far too late. Caroline was working early, so we headed home. Geordie had arranged for Joe to pick us all up from the Bohemian. It was agreed that he would drop Geordie and Sheena first, and then drive to Putney before ending up in Streatham. Geordie and Sheena exchanged knowing glances when Caroline asked if Joe could drop both me and her at her Putney flat.

When Caroline and I eventually arrived at the flat, there was an answerphone message from Caroline's hospital, asking her to go in if she was able. Caroline rang the ward back and was told that two colleagues had been taken ill and they were short-staffed. They were desperate for help. I knew that Caroline would not delay going in for a moment.

I suggested that she get changed whilst I organised a taxi for her. The hospital was on Fulham Palace Road, only 13 minutes for Caroline if she went on her bike, and so she insisted on cycling.

As Caroline changed, she confessed that being always available had meant that the hospital took advantage of her. She felt they almost ran with fewer staff than they needed because she was so reliable.

I apologised if I was taking too much of her time and she came over and kissed me.

She told me that on the contrary, she wanted to spend more time with me and was sorry she had to leave.

I so wished I had my bike. I found myself worried about her cycling so late at night, especially as she was tired and had been out. She assured me that she had done the journey a thousand times before she had met me and the chances were that she could catch up on some sleep if the shift went quiet.

I watched her go. This was a girl that caused me pain every time she left me. I was not going to ever let her leave my life, that was for certain. I had a tea as coffee kept me awake but I still struggled to sleep. I was thinking about Haston but it was Caroline that I could not get out of my mind.

*As for Mrs Eischrank; she had thirteen girls.*

## Attachment 28

## Deviation

*Records tell that Captain Cook was prone to losing his keys, and so he kept them in the compass housing of his ship* HMS Endeavour. *Whilst magnetic compasses had been used for over 1,000 years, they have only recently been understood. Certainly, Captain Cook never realised how much deviation his keys may have caused to his compass.*

*Deviation occurs in biology as well as geology. A piece of grit in an oyster creates the pearl. It therefore seems reasonable that the same principles can, and should, work in life.*

*People need to sit back and ask themselves why "life" works. Is it because everything is perfect or are some elements a problem? It may well be that part of our lives works better because it is out of kilter or is a problem. How many times does a new "upgrade" fail to live up to expectation or a "time-saving" technology require greater manpower and time? It always makes good sense not to repair something that does not need fixing. But it takes a wise person to know when to do nothing.*

*The same principles apply to others. Apart from weight loss, gardening and cookery, the bestselling non-fiction books are on "self-help". Whilst everyone is interested in what makes they themselves tick, too few are interested in understanding what makes others tick. The Greeks were the first to try. They formalised and popularised the "four temperaments" some 2,500 years ago and their theories persisted until the 1850s. Thereafter, Carl Jung started what was to become the science of personality. Briggs, Kersey, Eysenck and Birman and countless others all gave their names to methods of understanding personality. Psychometric testing is now commonplace and appraisals are meant to identify traits. Everyone seems to want to "get their best" out of themselves. But who says getting the best is important? Alexander Fleming failed to disinfect the culture he was working on and discovered Penicillin. Alfred Nobel accidentally dropped gun cotton in nitroglycerin and discovered gelignite. Charles Goodyear spilt sulphur onto rubber and discovered vulcanisation. The Kellogg Brothers made cornflakes quite unintentionally when they left cooked wheat for a day and then tried to roll it.*

*The list of inventions and discoveries that required a mistake, an error or a complete botch is enormous and includes among many others radioactivity, infrared, inkjet printers, microwaves and Uranus.*

*Maybe we need to identify the deviant, the messy, the clumsy or the irritant. They may be the star that can make life tick.*

*Sometimes you can get large rewards for little effort,*

*such as when ordering a pizza. Perhaps a little effort should be directed at getting things wrong. Who knows what discoveries may be made? Although they will probably not be as interesting as those made by Captain Cook. Now where did he put those keys?*

## Ryan Haston

It was gone six when the coffee shop started to close. I had eaten a tea cake, an Eccles cake and a piece of millionaire shortbread in my time killing time. My sugar levels were high, even if my spirits were low. I had another night to wait and was at a loss to know where to stay. I was starting to wonder if the hiding was necessary. *Did Robert care that much or was all this in my head?* Before I decided where to go and what to do, I left the café and found a phone box.

I tried phoning Steve, but he was not there and Quentin came on the phone. Quentin was keen to enquire about my mother. I genuinely could not remember what I had told Quentin so I had to be deliberately vague and bluff as I could not lie very well. I had to continue with the hollow platitudes saying how bad it had been and that I would rather not talk about it. What I wanted to ask about was if anyone was asking for me, but Quentin wanted to talk about how the revamp was going. Quentin was enthusiastic and starting telling me everything. Whilst this did deflect the issue with my mother, it did mean that I could not get a word in. I was running out of change for the phone and cut in on Quentin. I said I would be back in a couple of days if anyone needed me.

It was at this point that Quentin told me how I had been in demand. On the night I left, a man was looking for me and he returned on the following night, which Quentin thought must have been the Friday, and on the Saturday, four friends came, planning to watch me perform. I asked who they were, but Quentin could not remember. The doorman thought the first man that came with a driver was called Robert.

I had to say, 'Bye', as the pips had gone.

I felt somewhat pleased that I had not been delusional. Robert was still very interested in what I was up to. Robert knew about both Lela's and the Madam YoJo flat. He knew about Stein and so I presume he knew all about Shawcross now. I was faced with another night in a grotty B&B. *Or was I?* I thought that, as I was not short of money, I would live in style so I took a cab to the St Ermine's Hotel. I had a vague recollection that my father had always stayed in the St Ermine's when he came to London on business. When I saw the plush decoration and the quality of the hotel, I thought it was more likely that it was where he and Glenna stayed. Once in my room, I drew a bath and had a long soak before a long sleep.

In the morning, I was able to have a power-shower and

a shave with a new hotel razor. After a full breakfast, I went to see Mark, who was, as usual, more than helpful. I asked him to be discreet and he assured me that he was bound by client confidentiality and I should have no concerns on that score. I then headed back to Victoria by Tube ready to face the Post Office. I had been prepared for more hassle and was delighted that within 20 minutes, and twelve pounds poorer, I had my British Visitor's Passport. It was in the name of Ryan V Haston, unlike my equity card. Mark had my details from when the Edward Hardy Trust was established and was able to provide me with a certified copy of my original driving licence. Mark also advised me that as I had lost my actual Sean Cross passport, I could not get a BVP, but would need to apply for a replacement. Mark had explained that he was not a lawyer who dealt with passports but hoped that it all made sense. I was delighted. The trip to the ferry was uneventful. I was a day later than I had anticipated, but re-joined the queue in the terminal ready for my crossing to France.

As I looked forward along to the entrance door, the ferry operative checking tickets and passports was the self-same smiling Simon Cross. I was initially pleased, as I had built up a rapport. I then broke into a mild sweat. Simon's rapport was with Sean Cross.

'Bugger, bugger!' I cursed myself for being so prominent the day before. I was now Ryan Haston. How would I explain the change of names without arousing attention? As I stood in despair, a girl touched my arm. I jumped and yelped.

It was a tall, blonde girl, who stepped back and said, 'Sean, whatever is the matter?'

I sighed and explained that I had been miles away as this was not my ferry. The girl was Val McMahon, who had trained with me at LAMDA and was now telling me she was working in Paris. Val questioned me as to why it was not my ferry.

Thinking on my feet, I explained that my colleague, who I was waiting for, had not turned up and so I had decided to wait until the next ferry. Val suggested that I travel over with her, and I could wait in Calais.

The queue was moving forward, and I was trying to escape without making a scene nor be noticed by Simon, but Val was trying to get my phone number and did not want to let me go. Eventually I stepped out of the queue with my back to Simon and wrote my number on the back of the only piece of paper I had, which was the code to the safe. Val seemed disappointed, but satisfied. As I walked back from the queue, she shouted after me, 'Sean, Sean'. For a moment, I was tempted to ignore her and walk on, but I stopped and she had caught up with me. 'You have my pen!' I was still holding the rather smart silver ballpoint pen she had given me to write down my number. I blushed. Val laughed, kissed me on the cheek and told me I was a kleptomaniac. I looked up to Simon who was checking documents at the front of the queue, he had not seen me and was pre-occupied with his tasks.

As it turned out, I had to miss the next ferry as well, before Simon went off shift or at least was not on duty at the entrance. It was two of the longest hours of my life. The ferry terminal is not designed for long term occupation, especially if you are trying to keep a low profile. I read a newspaper and tried to do the crossword. It would have been useful to have kept Val's pen for the task. Nevertheless, I was able to board the ferry without any problem. I will never know, but I did wonder what would have happened if Sean Cross had tried to board. *Would he have been taken into a side room for questioning and anything he was carrying searched and maybe confiscated?*

I was amazed at how quickly I was in Dusseldorf. The crossing had been calm and stress free. The trains ran exactly to timetable, not that I had looked at a timetable. I was just grateful to have escaped from England. The train was wonderful to Lille and then onto Eindhoven in Holland. I had some time to wait in Eindhoven before my connecting train to Venlo on the Dutch border. I was then able to get a direct, fast, comfortable express straight to Dusseldorf. I was too late to change trains for Bielefeld and too late to get a taxi, so I spent the night in Dusseldorf at the Hotel Rheinischer Hof. I had a tiny room, but the staff were friendly and it was a stone's throw from the station.

As I expected, the hotel took my passport on arrival and I presumed it was kept in the safe. Whilst it was too late for the train, it was too early for bed, so I strolled into Dusseldorf. The area around the station was, like in most European cities, a little sordid. The bars were louder and more boisterous than I had expected for a mid-week night.

After trying a beer in a bar full of Turkish workers where no-one spoke German, I left and went down the steps into a dark cabaret club called the Parisienne. I was surprised how empty it was and decided to leave, when I was joined by a scantily clad lady who asked me to buy her a drink. I struggled to work out her age, but it was at least twice mine, and she seemed unaccompanied. She was brandishing a bottle of cheap Sekt. I realised that it was not the type of cabaret club I was expecting. My new friend took hold of my hand as I tried to leave. I broke her grip and apologised telling her I had to go.

She seemed crestfallen so I smiled and said, 'Maybe next time,' with just a hint of Liza Minnelli, which I knew Stein would have appreciated, even if the Fraulein had not. I went to the steps, where the burly doorman stopped me. He insisted that I could not leave until I had paid for the lady's drink that I had bought her. I had neither the will nor the inclination to argue. I was relieved of 100 Deutsche Marks for my naivety. I went back to the hotel angrier and poorer, but wiser.

I was still annoyed with myself next morning, but cheered up when I caught the train to Bielefeld. The train was spotless, arrived on time and I was served a hot coffee almost as I sat down. I decided that I was going to enjoy the German railways. They were clean, fast and never crowded and I arrived on time in Bielefeld. I took an off-yellow German taxi to the barracks. It was a Mercedes, and not unlike the Mercedes used by Robert. This was some comfort to me, as I thought British Intelligence would never use a black Mercedes. Robert was definitely dodgy. The taxi could not pull into the Kaserne, as the gates were closed. I alighted and walked with the parcel to the entrance. I noticed that whilst there were soldiers in uniform on the gate, the guard room reception had civilians as well as soldiers. I walked to the first window and asked to speak to Captain Jacobs. I was asked for Captain Jacobs' branch or department by a man with two stripes on his arm. His name tag said Corporal Jones and I wondered how many people had said, 'Don't panic, don't panic!' to him. I was distracted by my thoughts and the corporal had to repeat the question.

I confessed that I did not know.

The corporal said no worries and proceeded to read through a directory and then made a phone call. He spoke to someone and then directed me to a chair inside the waiting room. He invited me to take a seat until the captain arrived. He asked me if I was intending to enter the barracks, and if so, I should start filling in the form which was attached to one of the many clipboards on the table. I was keen to escape once I had delivered the parcel, so declined.

After what seemed only a few moments, Captain Jacobs bounced in and said, 'Tuva! I believe you have a package for me.' I had no idea who or what Tuva was, but assumed it was the bouncy officer's cry of exclamation. I was the only person in the guardroom and there could be no misunderstandings, so I stood up and meekly offered the parcel. Captain Jacobs raised his hands and said, 'Sorted!' and bounced out.

I cursed myself for paying off the taxi because once I was outside, I realised that I was stranded. I went back into the guard room and asked the corporal if he could order me a taxi.

He asked me how I had arrived, and I replied, 'By taxi.' He gave me a wry grin. He did not need to say anything, but I knew what he was thinking.

He said that the lay-by opposite was a bus stop and towards the front was a taxi rank.

I did not have to wait long before I was able to grab another off-yellow Mercedes and this time, I ordered the driver to go straight to Dusseldorf Haupt Bahnhof. It took almost four hours because of the traffic around Essen in the Ruhr Valley. Essen really was the heart of West Germany's industry. Factories spread for miles as all the cities and towns joined together, making for a quite depressing journey. The taxi took twice as long as the train journey would have taken. When I eventually arrived at the station, I was disappointed to note that the train to Calais that I had arrived on did not seem to have an equivalent the other way. The best way was to get the train to Arnhem and then to Lille the following day.

I had never been to Arnhem, and this was my chance to do so. It had been my "longest day" and I felt a night on the Lower Rhine was appropriate. I did tell myself that I couldn't use the "longest day" as my description, as that was D-Day. I should have used *A Bridge Too Far*, *A Bridge Too Far* being the film of the operation by the Allies to take the bridge at Arnhem to accelerate the end of World War II. I was minded that I was starting to talk to myself but as I had now carried out my task, I could treat the rest of this trip as a holiday.

I was fascinated by Arnhem. I found a strange tranquillity, standing by the river. I did wish I had someone to stand with me at moments like this. I did not speak Dutch, but my command of German and knowledge of Indo-European languages allowed me to read the pamphlet that I had picked up at the station.

Arnhem was the location of a major battle of World War II. It was the concluding part of what was a failed attempt to cross the Lower Rhine as part Operation Market Garden.

The Allies had planned to enter the Dutch town after sweeping through France and Belgium in the summer of 1944, after the Battle of Normandy. Market Garden was intended to be a single line of attack over the Lower Rhine River, allowing the British Second Army to bypass the heavily defended German position known as the Siegfried Line and attack into the Ruhr.

I had just driven through the Ruhr. I shook my head and tried to imagine what it must have been like in the 1940s. I read on.

Allied paratroopers were dropped in the Netherlands to secure key bridges and towns along the Allied axis of advance. In the far north, the 1st Airborne Division, a British Division, landed at Arnhem to secure the bridges, one of which is now known as Pegasus Bridge. As well as those landing by parachute, forces were delivered by gliders of the Glider Pilot Regiment. It was planned that the main thrust of ground forces would reach the bridges within two to three days.

Unfortunately, the paratroopers landed quite a long way from the bridges, and they also met fierce resistance that they had not anticipated. Germans of the 9th and 10th SS Panzer Divisions had been resting in the area. Only a small force was able to reach the Arnhem road bridge, while the main body of the Division was halted on the outskirts of the town. The force that was moving to relieve them was stopped on the route to them due to heavy fighting. After four days, the overwhelmed paratroopers were forced to withdraw to a small pocket on the north of the river. The bridge was overwhelmed, and the rest of the Division became trapped in a confined area, where they could not be reinforced by land, nor by the RAF's flights. After nine days of fighting, the broken remnants of the Division were withdrawn. The Allies were unable to advance further, with no secure bridges over the Lower Rhine, and the front line stopped south of Arnhem.

As I was standing by the river, I was conscious of an old couple standing behind me. As I turned to leave, I said instinctively, 'Guten morgen' in German instead of "Goedemorgen", the Dutch. The couple answered in German and asked if I was German. Given my blue eyes and blond hair, people often asked if I was Scandinavian or German so it came as no surprise.

I explained that I was British and just visiting. I asked the couple if they were having a good day. Whilst hesitant to start with, and in a broken English, they explained they had come from Stuttgart. The husband had spent his seventeenth birthday at Arnhem, and they came back every decade to remember his fallen comrades and the other young men on what they called "the other side of the river". I stood in silence with them for some little time. Nothing was said, we just all cried together.

I ended up staying one night in Arnhem and then

retreating back to Stein's flat the following day. I was an arrogant, privileged, entitled man who needed to get his life back on track.

## Attachment 29

## The Ties that Bind

*Life expectancy in the UK has reached its highest level on record for both men and women. A newborn baby boy can expect to live for 77.4 years and a newborn baby girl 81.6. This is in stark contrast to Eswatini (Swaziland), where people live on average less than 40 years. Whilst we take our good fortune for granted, it is worth remembering that a mere 100 years ago, our life expectancy would have been between 30 and 45. So what are we doing with our extra time? The answer is probably very little. Our forebears were governed by the seasons and daylight, but we are supposedly a 24-hour society. Yet the reality is that we now get up later and end the working day earlier, usually to collapse in front of our 50-inch plasma screens. We start work later in our lives, have significantly more leisure time and we retire earlier. Our grandparents left education at 14 and our own children nearer 24, following a "gap year" and university. Our grandparents had fewer holidays, usually two weeks per year. Christmas Day was not a holiday in Scotland until 1957! Our great-grandparents worked mainly on the land or in heavy industry with little aid from technology. Even household chores were time and energy consuming. The first vacuum cleaner was not patented until 1901 and that was by a British man.*

*Hoover did not get a patent until 1908 and that was for the rotating brush at the end. In fact, life at the turn of the 20th century was, to quote Hobbes,* nasty, brutish and short.

*So, if you are likely to die early, it is important that you get everything done sooner, as you cannot delay. Alexander the Great ruled the greatest part of the ancient world at a mere 33 years old. Mozart was a child prodigy and it was just as well, as his life was tragically short – he died aged 35.*

*There are, of course, some remarkable exceptions. The Sistine Chapel ceiling was painted by Michelangelo between 1508 and 1512, when he was 71. So here is the maths. Take your current age from 77 if you are a man, and 81 if you are a woman. The figure you are left with is the likely time you will have to conquer the world. Alternatively, you might decide to start getting up earlier, enjoying the day more, going to bed later and possibly learning to paint.*

## Gordon

Caroline, Geordie, Sheena, and I never did get back to the Bohemian burlesque bar. Geordie and Sheena were married in probably the lowest key ceremony that they have ever seen at a registry office in Edinburgh, Sheena's hometown. There were no guests. Geordie was adamant that no-one should be forced to enjoy what was going to be his and Sheena's greatest day together. They adopted two children, one of whom, Caroline's godson, had severe learning difficulties. I asked Geordie to be my best man when I got married to Caroline. Geordie reminded me that he was only accepting because he was never asked anywhere. He placed one condition on the acceptance. That condition was that he could nominate someone to make the best man speech for him. I agreed to his bizarre request, thinking he would ask Caroline's brother, Mark, but he selected Haston.

I had seen Haston twice since I "burgled" his friend's flat and was accused of treason. On the first occasion, I was returning from the squash club, and we waved across Earl's Court Tube station platforms, and the second was a prearranged meal in Shepherd's Bush, following a long letter that he had sent me, and I can't for the life of me now find. The letter was an explanation for his actions and with a full and wholesome apology. It was in the first person and it ran to eight separate parts, that I copied into my version of events. I curse myself because I have lost the original letter as I believed, and still believe, that one day Haston will be famous and the letter will be a prized exhibit of some museum. The letter was a gripping read, and I fully understood the reason why I had been lured into his web. I cannot churn out the letter here, but Haston's opening lines were not Shakespeare but E.M. Forster.

*'One minute. You know nothing about him. He probably has his own joys and interests, wife, children, snug little home. That's where we practical fellows',* he smiled, *'are more tolerant than you intellectuals. We live and let live, and assume that things are jogging on fairly well elsewhere, and that the ordinary plain man may be trusted to look after his own affairs.'*

I have read and re-read the start and maybe it is because I am not an intellectual, but I cannot work out if I am the ordinary plain man he mentions.

Following the letter, we met at The Hat Shop. The Hat Shop was a restaurant in Shepherd's Bush, but from the outside seemed to anyone passing by, to be just that, a hat shop. I had been minded to invite Caroline or even Geordie and Sheena to join us, but I had so many questions that I needed to ask, it was, I thought, best to go alone. In retrospect, whilst it was a great meal, the letter had answered so many of the questions that I had been itching to ask that we ended up discussing Quentin, Steve, Gino from the Bohemian and of course Stein. Haston was so pleased that I had been as he called it "thrilled rotten" by the episode. He told me he would have Stein and Quentin provide their recollections of their role in the drama.

Our wedding was in a marquee in the garden at Caroline's parents' house. Caroline's father apologised to me in his speech for being rude to me the first time we met. He went on to explain to the gathered guests that his behaviour to me that night could be explained because of the performance of one man who had been the villain of the piece. He was then able to introduce that self-same villain, who he was prompted to call "the man of all names and all seasons, Jaffa Haston."

Haston's speech was terrific. I say speech, but he started by singing without any accompaniment, *Wilkommen*. We had named all the guests tables after Tube stations and places where Caroline and I had memories. These included Putney, Streatham and Wandsworth. Haston had noted them down and during his speech he would, at random times, direct compliant guests from one station to another, thereby neatly shuffling the table plan. Everyone, including my mother-in-law, was amused. Haston, in a mock Geordie accent, commented on her 'beautiful green frock' which was actually a salmon colour. Everyone laughed, but no-one as loudly as Geordie. Haston was such a performer. Every one of Caroline's single friends and even some of the married ones fell in love with him. Male and female.

Haston never married but retained his good looks and charm. A week before my wedding, Haston came to stay. He seemed to want one night to get to know me better before he took on the task of standing in for Geordie. He was using the wedding and our meeting as the bookends of a tour of the North East which started in York and the Minster. He planned to visit Jervaulx, Rievaulx, Bolton and Fountains Abbeys. He particularly wanted to visit Durham Cathedral, then he was heading up to Lindisfarne. He said that whilst he had not found religion, he had found a hobby. He was collecting church architecture. We had sat outside a pub on the village green for most of a balmy afternoon. The same green where two decades earlier, we had slept, wrapped in a tent. I reminded Haston how much we had cursed him that night. He laughed, remembering how he woke up in hospital with the tent poles. He did say that sleeping rough had influenced his life, as he now helped with a homeless charity running a soup kitchen twice a month.

We then retreated to the house, where we continued to drink. It was a strange melancholic day and evening. Haston did confess to me, on that night, that he might have been homosexual but was never brave enough to find out. On the same night, he filled me in with the gaps in the story face to face. He said his letter was impersonal and just gave the facts but could not convey his feelings. I did point out that any letter that started with a quote from *Howard's End* was very personal. Whilst he felt really bad about drawing me into the plot, he knew that I was absolutely the man to trust. He was in a situation that he could not control and luckily once the parcel was delivered, he could think straight again. Mention of the parcel made him pause and raise a finger almost like a cricket umpire. He reached down into the pocket of his jacket that he had thrown down beside his chair. He gave me an envelope. I opened it. Haston said that it was the last piece of the puzzle that I had asked for. There were, what appeared to be typed witness statements from Stein and Quentin and a further paragraph from him. Quentin's was in a strange font.

'I hope that answers all the questions?' he offered. He explained that on return from Europe, he had gone back to the Bohemian as if nothing had happened. He helped with some of the revamp and rehearsed the new show, *The Shaming of the Few*. Haston said that despite Quentin's planned radical change, it was essentially the same format with the same characters and their acts had not changed much. His German rendition of *Where have all the flowers gone* could not capture the mood evoked by Marlene Dietrich, and was soon quietly replaced by *Mack the Knife* in German. The bar was better stocked, but had not moved position, as Steve's proposed layout would have reduced the seating numbers, and so was shelved very early on. The building was freshly painted and everyone was happy, so all was well that ended well.

I did have one matter that I asked him to explain with and that was Robert. Haston told me that Robert may have been the man in glasses at the Pimlico house, so strangely enough I might have met him when arrested for treason. Haston had particularly impressed Robert, who he called his "handler". Far from being upset or angry, Robert was delighted by Haston's behaviour. Haston had been confronted by an enthusiastic Robert and taken for a coffee. Robert was pleased with Haston's ingenuity and verve, despite the fact that it had delayed Robert's report to the Cabinet. Robert had, as he had explained to Haston, simply been checking Stein's suitability for the high office that he was to subsequently achieve. Robert wanted Haston to work for him more than ever. Haston declined, or at least he thought he had declined, but that as Haston pointed out, he did not want to work with them from the outset.

As the night grew longer and the drink was talking, he told me he had passed some initiation ceremony and was now a "Fly". He told me the Flies were bonded by a tattoo. I told him that I was in the Rotary and bonded by a tie and a lapel badge. I do not recall anything further.

## Attachment 30

## Landing

**Ryan Haston**

I did not see Stein immediately when he came back from Ireland, as I was working full time. After several days, I left him a note saying that we should try and meet on the Monday evening for a video. He wrote on the same note that he would be there. I had planned to put on *Carousel* but in the event, we ended up just chatting. Stein was anxious to tell me that whilst Marta had been "returned home to Estonia", it was under direction because she was more useful in Estonia, where events were turning, than she was in Cheltenham. Stein could not tell me the full story for "obvious" reasons, just like I could not tell Stein my full story for "obvious" reasons. Stein was able to say that his enquiries into Marta had led back to Mr Robert Harold. There were some red faces in the Ministry, given Mr Harold's new target… was Stein himself!

Stein quoted Brutus, '*There is a tide in the affairs of men, which taken at the flood leads on to fortune.*'

I finished the quote, '*Omitted, all the voyage of their life is bound in shallows and in miseries.*' I thanked Stein for not saying *et tu, Brute*.

Stein said on the contrary, he had been impressed the lengths that I had gone to in order to protect him. He had never felt betrayed. Indeed, he had received that pat on the back he had been promised and I could read about it in *The Times* when the Queen's Birthday honours were published.

I did go down to Frome to meet Jocasta and the girls. I became Uncle Jaffa, their favourite uncle. I introduced them to the theatre and I was a popular member of the Stein Gilbert and Sullivan Group, who would gather in the drawing room and sing along to the Victorian operettas. I was also a useful tennis player (according to Jocasta) and Jocasta and I always made the girls work for their victory. I eventually moved to the West Country and I helped finance a cabaret theatre in Bristol that Quentin established. I did some charity work. My greatest achievement was to present a series of documentaries highlighting the homeless and other social problems. Quentin and Stein wrote a book together on cabaret and both Stein and I became honorary Flies. I am not sure whether Stein would have had to disclose his tattoo to his political masters. I only ever told Shawcross.

# Attachment 31

**Gordon Shawcross**

Caroline and I first moved into the Old Vicarage to look after her ageing father when her mother died. There was plenty of room, but it was so expensive to run. We rented out the London flat, which gave us a second income. Caroline took a consultant post at Darlington Hospital and I just did insurance. As a way of supplementing my income, I had considered two options; one was to lecture at an evening class on economic theory, the alternative was to edit a technical journal on re-insurance. I could not decide which would be the least boring and ended up doing them both.

In the most part, I was a "stay at home dad" for Heidi and Raich. I know I can get tiresome when I talk about my children, but I shall explain their names. Caroline was interested in her family tree. She didn't need the Old Rectory to give her a backstory like her parents. The Jervises were originally Jermakovs, who were Estonians of Russian stock. Caroline's great-grandmother was Heidi and was evicted from her settlement during one of the many pogroms. Heidi had walked all the way from a village near Tartu to Esbjerg in Denmark, some 1,800 kilometres. It had taken almost two months. On arrival, she had met Horatio, another émigré from Vara, the next village to hers, in Estonia. It was their son who came to

England and was Caroline's grandfather. Our son is Simon Horatio, we call him Raich, I wanted him to be just Horatio but was not brave enough. I am comfortable that given their names and backgrounds both he and Heidi will have interesting lives. Caroline and I often talk of re-walking the route from Estonia to Esbjerg and inviting Haston to be our interpreter and guide.

The Edward Hardy Trust made a bequest to his old polytechnic (which had now been granted university status) to improve the teaching of the performing arts. Haston had stood down as a Trustee and now I was "up north", I stepped in. It meant I saw Geordie at least once a year at board meetings.

It was whilst sitting in what we now always call the Orangery, reading *The Times* on a cold Wednesday in November, that the obituary of Sir A P Stein caught my eye. He had had a distinguished career in the Civil Service and had received his knighthood, which was attributed to his careful steering of the Labour government towards a new general code for sexual conduct in the armed forces. The obituary was at pains to point out Sir Anthony was married with twin girls – Rosie, a lawyer, and Gina, an actress. Sir Anthony was described as eclectic; being both an expert on Mendelssohn and the co-author of a book on cabaret and burlesque with the theatre impresario Quentin McCrae. Sir Anthony, as Chair of the Anglo-Russian Cultural Society, had also fostered a close relationship with the St

Petersburg cultural society run by his friend the Russian Oligarch Sergei Agafonov.

His greatest contribution had been his, undisclosed at the time, but much heralded, co-ordination of the government's response to East Germany during the period of the fall of the Berlin Wall. The chain of events that led to the fall of the wall could be traced back to the demonstrations outside the St Nicholas Church in Leipzig, fermented by a group based at the church. *The Times* noted that Sir Anthony, a polyglot, was in regular contact with the group as a committed Christian. It mentioned his wife's expertise in theology, her books and their shared passions. The final paragraph noted that Stein loved the film *Cabaret* and told friends that when he died, he wanted to *go like Elsie* – but they had no idea if he had. I thought that there was so much that *The Times* did not know, but then I only knew because of Haston. Haston would have known.

Sitting reading the obituary, I thought maybe I should write a book on Haston's adventures and my starring role. I already had a title – *Agent Orange*. As I was musing, the palms behind me separated and I felt the loyalty, honesty, charity, diligence, patience, humility, and kindness flood through. I then heard…

'Very interesting… but stupid!'

# About the Author

Bryan Campbell Johnston was raised and schooled in North Yorkshire, then returned with his wife, Wendy, to live in Richmondshire in 2020. Bryan has three children, two step-children and he and Wendy have five grandchildren.

Between leaving North Yorkshire and returning, Bryan had both a military and legal career. His military career started at Royal Military Academy Sandhurst and ended as a Major commanding an infantry company during Gulf War I. In between, he served in Germany and Northern Ireland and other outposts around the shrinking globe.

His legal career started at The University of Westminster and the School of Law, and ended as a solicitor and managing partner of a law firm. In between, Bryan was involved in the arts as a director and trustee of a regional theatre for six years. He has been, among other appointments, chair of a charity and chair of a chamber of commerce. Bryan is a trained mediator.

Bryan wrote articles for a business magazine for several years; he had a play performed at Brentwood Theatre and his adaptation of *Northanger Abbey* was performed in over 31 locations by a professional touring troupe.

Bryan's hobbies include writing, theatre, horseracing, sailing, golf, trekking and skiing. Bryan writes under the name Campbell Johnston and *Horace* was his first published novel.

xxvdesertrat

Bluesky @desertratxxv.bsky.social

http://alqo.co.uk

https://instagram.com/campbell_johnston_author

email: Campbell@alqo.co.uk

www.blossomspringpublishing.com

Printed in Dunstable, United Kingdom